Liberty Belle

The Snowberry Series Book 5

Katie Mettner

Copyright © 2015 Katie Mettner

All rights reserved

The characters and events portrayed in this book are fictitious. Any similarity to real persons, living or dead, is coincidental and not intended by the author.

No part of this book may be reproduced, or stored in a retrieval system, or transmitted in any form or by any means, electronic, mechanical, photocopying, recording, or otherwise, without express written permission of the publisher.

ISBN-10 : 151418723X
ISBN-13 : 978-1514187234

Cover design by: Art Painter
Library of Congress Control Number: 2018675309
Printed in the United States of America

Dedication:

For every person who lives with a chronic illness.

Prologue

Three years earlier

"In other news, Mayo Clinic in Rochester reports…" I slammed my hand down on the snooze button and moaned. It was too early for news, and much too early to be awake.

"Time to make the donuts, Liberty," I muttered, rubbing my hands over my face as I sat on the edge of the bed.

Well, in my case, it was time to make the pies, but that wasn't how the commercial went. The coffee pot came on and started its morning gurgling. Next, I would hear Dad moving about as he got ready to go, too. At three a.m., we didn't exactly have to worry about heavy traffic in Snowberry. Our commute only took a few minutes to get down to our bakery, the Liberty Belle.

I stood up and stretched, my back tight from the busy few days we had last week. We booked three weddings the first week of May and getting all those cakes baked, decorated, and delivered on time was a lesson in planning and luck. Thankfully, the brides and grooms had a beautiful May day for their big event, and I wasn't rained on while carrying cakes in and out.

I stuck my head around the corner of my bedroom door and called down the hall, "Dad, time to get up!"

After giving him a wakeup call, I went to the bathroom to wash, my eyes still partially closed. I moaned when the warm washcloth settled on my face, and I held it there until the cloth cooled. I hung it to dry, then threw on my white baker's uniform and hopped down the hall while tugging on my favorite tennies. I hopped past Dad's room on my way to the coffee pot and stopped. The door was cracked, but the room was still dark. I pushed it open a little bit further and noticed his bed was empty.

"Dad?" I called as I skidded to a stop in the open kitchen and living area.

The house remained quiet and I checked the other rooms, my heart tapping out a staccato knocking against my ribs. Where was he, and why didn't he leave a note?

I threw the door open to the garage and sighed with relief when his car was gone. He must have left for work early, and didn't want to wake me.

I grabbed my phone and sent him a text saying I was on my way. Then I filled my travel mug, switched the coffee pot off, and hesitated at the door to the garage. It was spring now and the weather was nice and warm. Since Dad was already at the bakery, there was no rush. Walking the few blocks to Main Street would work some of the kinks out of my body from the last few days. I grabbed my house key, instead of my car key, and went out the side garage door, basking in the warmth that greeted me, even at this time of the day.

The street lights lit my way as I walked up the street toward the bakery. Only in a town like Snowberry could a twenty-something woman walk alone at three a.m. without fear. I checked my phone, expecting a text back from Dad. There was nothing except my sent text saying delivered but not read. He must be busy on the bench. I stepped my speed up a bit, wanting to get there and help him as much as I could.

Since Mom died two years ago, he had thrown himself into his work at the bakery. He eats and sleeps marketing and new products, which will keep the Liberty Belle going for the next several generations. He knows I want to take over the business eventually, and is determined to hand it over to me in prime fiscal shape.

While he did that, I spent two years as a baker's apprentice then graduated to master baker, all while taking night classes in business and finance. I was ready, but he wasn't. Dad was using the business as a way to avoid an empty, lonely house. I understood how much he missed Mom. She was a vibrant woman, always smiling and sharing a kind word. I'm not sure how many people truly loved our donuts, and how many simply stopped in to chat with her.

Mom and Dad were ready for retirement, making plans to hand over the bakery to its namesake when she crashed her car one morning on the way to work. That's when everything changed. I wrapped my arms around my chest, my travel mug warm against the tender underside of my arm. The doctors think she may have passed out, hit the gas, and launched the car into the lake. No one noticed her until Dad went looking and found her car.

I shivered the same way I always do when I think about it. That phone call was a nightmare I relived over and over every time the phone rang. I wondered how long it would take before that feeling went away, but two years later, my heart still raced when my phone rang.

I rounded the corner onto Main Street and found myself jogging toward the storefront. The awning hung off the display window like always, its red and white fabric flapping lightly in the wind. A light shone from the back of the bakery where Dad was working. The warm glow lessened my anxiety as I put my key in the door and walked into the quiet storefront. There was no whomp-whomp of the steel mixer and no sizzling from the donut fryer. I turned and locked the door before I called out to him.

"Dad, I'm here. Why didn't you wake me up this morning?"

I grabbed a crisp, clean white apron from the box near the bakery cases and tied it around my waist, something I'd done a million times since I was a little girl, then carried my travel mug to the baker's bench. It was clean. There was no flour, no donuts, no bread dough rising, and no sign that anyone had been in. I looked around and was surprised that the mixer was still clean, and the proofer was off.

I pulled the cooler open, sticking my head inside, but it was as it was last night when I closed the bakery.

"Dad!" I called frantically, a sudden feeling of dread gripping my stomach. "Dad, where are you?"

Maybe he got a delivery and was unloading inventory. I rounded the area behind the cooler, where we stored our flour and sugar bags, along with tubs of frosting and boxes of bakery containers. I sighed with relief when I saw him resting on the flour bags.

"Dad, why don't you go home and go back to bed? I'll get things started here," I said, walking over to where he rested. His face was relaxed when I approached and I shook his shoulder. "Dad, wake up, you don't want to sleep here."

His head rolled when I shook him, and I knew instantly something was off. "Dad!" I yelled while I slapped his face lightly, but there was no response. I held my cheek near his lips, but they were cool and there was no air passing between them.

"Dad!" I cried, grabbing his hands. He didn't do anything but lie there, unmoving. Something slipped from his fingers and I picked it up, a sob catching in my throat. It was a picture of my mother smiling back at me.

I grabbed my phone and dialed 911.

"911, what's your emergency?" a voice asked.

I was crying and barely coherent. "It's my dad. I think he's dead!"

"Okay, honey, tell me where you are," came the voice over the line.

"I'm at the Liberty Belle. It's my dad, Jack. He's not breathing! I need an ambulance," I cried into the phone.

The slickness of the phone made it hard to hold it between my shoulder and ear while I held dad's hands.

"Okay, Liberty, I have a unit dispatched and on the way. Tell me what happened," she encouraged soothingly and calmly.

"I don't know! I just came into work and found him here on the flour bags. I don't know when he left home. It could have been hours ago. Should I do CPR?" I asked frantically, trying to move him off the flour bags to the floor. Sirens were faint as they came from the fire station on the other side of the lake.

"Check his neck for a pulse. Do you feel anything?" she asked calmly and I did what she asked but shook my head.

"No, there's no pulse, and he's not breathing. His lips are cold!"

"Liberty, listen to me, the ambulance is almost there. Is the door open for them?" she asked.

"No, I locked it when I came in because we

aren't open yet," I explained, my voice garbled with tears.

"Okay, leave your dad for a second and open the door, so the EMTs can get in," she ordered.

I ran through the bakery but didn't stop in time and slammed into the front door. I twisted the lock over just as I saw the lights of the ambulance reflected in the window.

"I can hear the sirens. Are the EMTs there?" she asked calmly.

"Yes, they just got here! Thank God!" I cried.

I hung up the phone as two men in blue uniforms ran toward me, carrying boxes. I led them to the back room, where my dad still lay in the same position.

"How long has he been down, Liberty?" the EMT asked.

"I don't know. I just found him like this five minutes ago. I don't know when he left home," I said quickly.

The one EMT held me back while the other checked him, looking for a pulse and checking his breathing. I noticed a subtle shake of his head and I wrenched out of the arms of the other EMT, kneeling next to my dad.

"Do something! Don't just sit there, do something!" I yelled.

The EMT turned to me and took my shoulders, shaking them firmly. "Liberty, he's gone. He's been gone for a few hours already. There is nothing I can do, honey."

I shook my head back and forth in slow motion, tears falling down my face. "No, no. No, he can't be dead," I whispered.

I laid my head on his chest and refused to let go.

Chapter One

Present Day

The bell above the door tinkled when someone entered the bakery. I stood up and stretched since the long hours of sitting to decorate cookies had left me stiff. I tried to stretch my right leg, but the new brace the docs hooked me up with wasn't cooperating. I checked my watch. It was barely eight a.m. and I had only opened the door a few minutes ago. Whoever was waiting in front of the bakery case had a real desire for donuts this Sunday morning.

I walked around the corner of the bakery wall to see the ringer of my bell. Bram Alexander stood in a suit and tie, bouncing on his toes. His shades were still on his face, the case of bread reflected in the overly polarized lenses.

"Hi, Bram," I acknowledged him, trying to step up on the stool to see over the case. The brace on my right leg hung me up, and I fell off, landing on my butt between the stool and the display case behind me.

"Liberty!" he exclaimed, then his shoes were in my line of sight. I was certain my cheeks were bright red when he bent down to check on me. "Are you okay?"

He offered his hand, so I took it and he hauled me up into a standing position again. "I'm fine," I lied. "I'm embarrassed but fine. I missed the step," I explained, motioning at the overturned stool.

"You use a stool to see over the case?" he asked, righting the offending block of wood. If he had noticed the white plastic and metal brace on my leg, he didn't let on.

"I've used that stool since I was ten and would come in to help dad when mom was too sick to come to work. If you hadn't noticed, I'm a wee bit vertically challenged," I teased, brushing off my white pants and straightening my frosting covered apron.

"You could look at it that way, but I like to look at it as being closer to the ground." He winked, and I blushed.

Bram Alexander was a year older, but not much taller than I was. His brother, Jay, was the Alexander in my yearbook. Bram certainly wasn't built like his brothers, Jake, Dully, and Jay. Even though Jay was in a wheelchair from Spina Bifida, he had guns that never quit, and sitting in his chair, he came up to Bram's ear. Bram reminded me of the runt of the litter. I tried to stifle the smile when my mind thought of that one. I was pretty sure he wouldn't appreciate me calling him a runt.

He stood before me, his face filled with concern, so I motioned around. "What can I get for you, Bram?"

"I'm here to pick up the cake for Snow and Dully," he answered, still watching me like a hawk. I wanted to say it was out of concern after the fall, but it felt like he was thinking about making me his breakfast.

I thunked my head with my hand. "Of course, the baptism!" I exclaimed. "I forgot it was today, but I do have the cake done. It's in the back, in a box. Let me get it from the cooler."

"Maybe I should help you carry it. I'm worried about that spill you just took," he said softly, as though he cared about my wellbeing. Bram Alexander caring about me was something that just couldn't happen, now or ever.

I brushed him off with my hand. "I'm okay, but it's a big cake, so if you want to carry it, that's fine with me."

I started back around the wall of the bakery, self-conscious knowing he could tell my right leg wasn't the same as my left. When I found out I had to wear this dumb brace, I bought a size bigger pants to hide it, but then I had to tighten the elastic, or they fell off. I was a hot mess, worse than the batch of pies in my industrial-sized oven. I stopped short and he bumped into the back of me. He grabbed my shoulders, his hands warm through my white t-shirt.

"Liberty?" he asked, and I hated the concern in his voice. I ignored it and turned around.

"Snow ordered the cake on the phone and I

haven't seen them since the baby was born. Do you have a picture? I'm dying to see her."

He grinned and pulled out his phone. "Are you kidding me? I'm her godfather and a photographer. Of course, I have pictures." He busied himself with his phone while I worked hard to ignore his charm.

The truth was, I was just buying time before I showed him the cake. His sister-in-law, Snow, is in a wheelchair after contracting polio as a baby. Suddenly, with him in my space, I was second-guessing my design on the cake. That shouldn't come as a big surprise to me. Bram Alexander always made me second guess myself, especially when I was turning down his invitations for a date.

"When Snow ordered the cake, she just gave me the baby's name and told me to take it from there. I've been so busy, I haven't had time to get over to see them," I explained.

He held up his phone, where there was a picture of a pink-faced cherub. She had bright blue eyes and was wrapped in a little yellow blanket. I took the phone and instinctively pulled it closer to my face. "She's so sweet," I sighed.

"She is. She's also very spoiled having Sunny as an older sister. She can't even peep and Sunny has a new diaper, pacifier, or is begging Snow to feed her," he laughed, shaking his head.

"Her name fits her," I said, handing the phone back.

"She's named after Snow's grandma who raised

her, Lila Jo. They had a hard time convincing Sunny that Dora wasn't the best name for her little sister. I think Lila Jo is a much better choice."

I laughed easily, picturing Sunny with her favorite Dora doll under her arm. "I can see her digging her heels in about that, but Sunny and Lila are perfect names. They go together like cupcakes and frosting. Speaking of frosting, we better get that cake." I took ten more steps and pulled the large walk-in cooler open and pointed at the box on the shelf.

He walked in and looked at it, then back to me. "It's absolutely gorgeous. You do such intricate work, Liberty. You're like an artist with frosting," he said, shaking his head in disbelief. He inspected the cake closer. "Did Snow bring those figures in? Wait, no, you just said you haven't seen her."

I motioned him out with the box. "Can't stand here cooling off the oven," I joked.

He set the box on my baker's bench and pointed at the figures on the cake again, his mouth opening and closing a few times. Here's the thing about the Alexander boys, they're too observant, especially this one. He's a photographer with the local paper and never misses a thing that goes on in this town, or about the people in it.

I set my hand on my hip. "No, Snow didn't bring them in, okay? I made them from marzipan. It's an old trick I learned from one of the finest," I informed him, so he would take the cake and be on his merry way. Unfortunately, he didn't budge.

"You made her wheelchair even," he said, still staring at the cake.

I rested the edge of my bottom on a stool. "She's in one, right?" I asked and he nodded. "I didn't figure it would make much sense to have a woman holding a baby near a baptismal font who was standing up. I'm not rude, Bram."

His head whipped toward me and he reached out, resting his hand on my shoulder. "No, that isn't what I meant at all, Liberty. I was just surprised at the detail and how much time and caring went into Lila's cake. I don't think any of us will want to eat it."

I laughed and stood up again, walking toward the front of the bakery. "I've heard that a thousand times, Bram. Don't worry, I can always make more. So please, eat it, and tell Snow, Dully, and the whole family how very happy I am for them. They deserve all the happiness their little family can give them. Also, be sure to tell them Lila Jo has a fairy cake-mother, just like Sunny does."

He stood at the door with his back to it, the cake in his arms, his head turned to the side. At some point, he had slipped his shades back on and I could see myself in the lenses. I looked nervous, to say the least. "You're the best, Liberty Belle. The absolute best."

I waved as he pushed the door open and left, the bakery silent again with his departure. It was Sunday, and the bakery was never busy until after church. I would have a rush of people dropping by for bread, rolls, and cookies, but then I would close for the day and enjoy some downtime at home.

My gaze traveled to the stool Bram had set up on all fours and grimaced. I was going to have to replace that. My right leg was officially done cooperating, and even without a final diagnosis, I knew that was never going to change.

What I was going to replace it with was the burning question. I'm too short to hand people cakes and pies without some sort of step. Replacing the cases wasn't an option considering how expensive they were, and I figured I wasn't going to grow any taller at the ripe old age of twenty-five. That only left one answer, a set of steps that were safe, and didn't get in the way for other less vertically challenged workers like my best friend, Lucinda. I guess I had better spend some time on the internet this afternoon.

I took a towel and glass cleaner to the fingerprint smudges on the glass around the small storefront. When my father, Jack Belle, opened this bakery twenty-four years ago, he was just starting out on his own as a baker. He came from the big city, having been trained by some of the best bakers in the business, to little Snowberry, Minnesota, where he knew this girl he couldn't get out of his heart. The rest, as they say, is history.

When his little girl was born, on the Fourth of July, they named her Liberty. Less than a year later, when he opened his own bakery, he named it *Liberty Belle*, after me. He always said there was no greater marketing tool than hearing someone say, "I'm heading over to the Liberty Belle, wanna join me?" He was right. This town has kept us in business for the last two decades.

The townspeople have seen us through the loss of my mother five years ago, and then my dad three years ago. The doctors say he had a massive heart attack, but I think he died of a broken heart. He never got over my mother dying so young.

He was gone, but I was still here, and I had to figure out a way to carry on his legacy, even with my current limitations. There were too many people in this town counting on me.

I checked the clock and noticed it was nearly nine a.m. I only had a few hours to get all the buns and breads bagged, and the cases filled before the folks started filing in. I stowed the glass cleaner and rag away. It was time to quit reminiscing and get on with the day.

Bram

The masterpiece in my arms was heavy; the weight of the cake a constant reminder to be very careful as I pushed out of the door and carried it to my SUV at the curb. I set it on the backseat, adjusting it just so to make sure it wouldn't slide around on the way back to Mom's house. Liberty's attention to detail tugged at my heart when my eyes drifted to the figure in the wheelchair again. Snow held a special place in our family, and now she had given us two precious little girls to love. Liberty did a fantastic job of honoring her with a little bit of frosting, and a whole lot of love.

I ducked out of the car door and closed it carefully, then turned back toward the bakery. I could see Liberty through the window, spraying and wiping the glass cases. Her back was turned to me and I took a moment to study her. She was the girl every boy wanted to date in high school, but she refused every offer. I couldn't figure out why, either. She was tiny but stunning. She was one of the few girls shorter than I was, but she was perfectly proportioned. I had spent more than my fair share of time trying to take her out on the town.

I jogged around the SUV, slid onto the seat, and pulled the door closed. As I turned the key over, my mind's eye pictured the scene a few moments ago of her falling to the floor. Something was off. Her gait was all wrong when she walked to the backroom, too. Her right leg was propelled by her dragging it with each step. One thing was certain; she was going to hurt herself if she kept trying to climb up on that stool. I lowered the gearshift to drive and checked my mirror before pulling away from the curb. I had an hour to get the cake back to Mom's and then join everyone at church, so I had best get a move on.

I turned and headed toward the place in which

I had grown up, and I thought about the wonderful people I had to support me. Liberty didn't have that. Her parents had both passed, her dad just a few years ago. She never missed a beat after his death, though. She only closed the bakery for the funeral and then went right back to work.

I hit the steering wheel with the palm of my hand and shook my head. Dammit! I thought I had that woman out of my system, but now she's running through my veins again. She will never let me take her out on a date, but I sure as hell was not going to let her hurt herself.

I pulled down the driveway to Mom's house and put my foot on the brake. I grabbed my phone from the cup holder and sent a text to the two guys I knew would help me.

It was official. Liberty Belle was once again the frosting on my cupcake.

Chapter Two

Liberty

The front display window revealed Bram Alexander walking down the Main Street, his camera around his shoulder, and his signature shades on his face. I had the urge to pull them off and see what was underneath, but I shook my head and sighed into the empty room. You know what's underneath, Liberty, sexy blue eyes that spent their entire senior year looking at you.

He must have seen me staring because he waved enthusiastically and I raised my hand back, feeling like a kid with her hand caught in a giant cookie jar.

I turned away and tried to pretend that I was rotating the loaves of bread, but I was actually hoping he just kept walking. It was three minutes until closing time and then I could escape out the back door, no one the wiser.

The bell tinkled over the door and I groaned inwardly. That bell has got to go. Now it's just getting on my nerves. I turned my head slowly to greet my customer, even though I was well aware it was him.

"Liberty," he said, grinning, his glasses tucked in his shirt by one bow.

"Bram," I answered, resting one fist on my hip. "It's just about closing time, but I have a few things left. What can I get you?"

He waved his hand a little at the case. "As much as I love your pie and donuts, I have to be careful, or I'll be sporting a donut belly," he teased, patting his stomach that was washboard flat.

I raised one brow. "Are you saying my wares are fattening?"

He nodded his head up and down like a puppet. "Absolutely, but man do they taste good going down. The baptism cake was so good. I had three pieces, and Dully made me do an extra lap around the property."

"Well, you deserved it if you ate three pieces. What brings you by if it isn't for sweet sugary confections?" I asked, before flipping the closed sign around on the door. My hand hesitated on the lock, but I didn't turn it just yet, no sense being locked in with the man.

"Something else just as sweet … you." He grinned but didn't miss a beat, leaving me no opening to object. "It's that time of year again for the summer business flyer. I thought with all the sprucing up you've done to the building, and the new display in the front window, I should take a new picture. I can leave everything else the same, insert the new picture, and bing, bang, boom, the Liberty Belle is in the flyer." He shook his camera a little with a grin on his face.

"Bing, bang, boom, huh?" I repeated, feeling like I was back in the 60's, instead of the current decade. He nodded and I swallowed nervously. His presence was enough to make me sweat even though it wasn't hot out. "Well ... um ... sure, I mean, I guess you can take a new picture. Do you need me to move the bread and cake display out of the window?"

He turned and checked the window display and then glanced back at me. "No, that's perfect. Do you have one of those frosting bag things?"

"Frosting bag things?" I asked, trying not to laugh at him. "You mean a pastry bag?"

"Is that what you call the thing the decorators put frosting in?" he asked and I nodded my head. "Okay, then yes, a pastry bag."

I went around the back of the bakery case and got one of my prefilled bags I use when customers need a quick, personalized cake to go. I held it up and tried to hand it over, but he refused to take it. Instead, he took me by the arm and led me to the window.

"Okay, now pretend like you're decorating the cake, and I'll get your picture from out front," he explained, pointing to the sidewalk.

"Oh, no." I backed up but ran smack dab into a rack of strudel. He caught my arm before I fell over and I shook him off. "I don't need to be in the picture. Just take it from the front and move along."

He laughed a long, slow, sexy, *you wish* kind of

laugh that made my insides a little like the jelly I infused in my bismarks. He set his camera down on the window ledge and leaned back, his ankles crossed. The Old Navy sweatshirt was stretched tightly across his chest, and his strong thighs were hidden by a pair of Wranglers, probably cowboy cut, if I cared enough to check, which I did not.

"People are drawn to action shots, Liberty. You have to give the people what they want," he pestered me, and I shook my head.

"The people want pies and bread, which I give them on a daily basis. They know who I am and what I do here. You know what? The old picture is fine. I'm closing now, so have a good day, Bram." I picked up my pastry bag and tried to push past him, but he caught my arm and did that laugh again. The laugh that made me wonder how it would sound in my bedroom, in the dark.

Dammit, Liberty, get a grip.

"Just one picture, babe. You'll love it, I promise. I'll even let you use it on your promotional materials if you want," he promised, crossing his heart.

"Babe? Do you call all your photo subjects *babe* to get them to do what you want?" I volleyed back.

His grin told me, yes, but his words defied that answer. "No, only the really sexy, fiery ones who refuse to cooperate."

"Bram Alexander!" I exclaimed, pushing him in the shoulder.

He grinned and laughed at the same time, an action that caused me to lose my battle with being mad. "Oh, alright, but only one picture." I shook my head at his little boy enthusiasm, then picked up the pastry bag and went back to the window.

He slung his camera over his shoulder, "Okay, one picture, but first …" he reached up and pulled off the hairnet I had over my blonde hair. It spilled out over my shoulders, and he moved some of it to fall across the front of my chest. "We make the people want you as much as your sweets."

Before I could say anything, he tugged me over to stand next to him. "Time to prime the camera."

"Prime the camera?" I asked, confused.

He held the camera up and out at arm's length. "Now, say selfie," he commanded, but I didn't. I just smiled primly like a third-grade teacher on picture day.

He checked the viewfinder and laughed. "We'll work on your selfie skills later."

He ducked out of the door before I could turn around and punch him, but I could still hear his laughter as he stood in front of the window. He was motioning for me to start pretending to decorate, so I did, but not before I stuck my tongue out at him.

He had the camera to his eye and was twisting the lens back and forth as I posed by the cake. If he thought I didn't know he was taking more than one picture, he was mistaken, but I sat through the torture anyway, just to have it over and done with.

He gave me a thumbs up and came back inside.

"You're a natural at this," he assured me, showing me the back of his camera. He clicked through about ten shots of me in various stages of decorating.

"You said one picture," I huffed, my hand on my hip.

He glanced up at me and nodded. "That is one picture. I used time-lapse, so technically, I didn't break my promise."

"You Alexander boys are all the same," I sighed, dashing behind the case to put away the pastry bag, and to get away from him.

"And how are we Alexander boys?" he asked from the door.

"Sneaky, but in a too nice kind of way. You're like a Catholic schoolboy controlled by the devil."

He started to laugh then, nearly hysterically, as he pulled out his phone and started to type. He was laughing so hard it was shaking in his hands, and it took him more than a minute to get himself under control.

"What are you doing?" I asked, grabbing the phone from his hand. He reached for it, but I held it above my head and shook it, "What are you doing?"

He wiped a tear from his eye. "I was texting my brothers what you just said. I wanted to brighten their day."

"Gah, you're infuriating!" I yelled, just as the phone chirped in my hand. I instinctively looked at the message. It was from Jay. "Jay says, right on, brother. Liberty has all of us pegged, don't ever forget that," I read it aloud then handed him the phone back.

He had the good sense to look sheepish.

I pointed at the phone. "He's right, and don't ever forget it."

He saluted me and slid the phone back in his pocket. "So, which picture did you like the best? I need to head back to the paper and get the insert put together before the end of the day."

I waved my hand around in the air. "I don't care. Use whatever one looks the best. I'm tired and need a nap."

"Wait, you're giving me permission to use whatever picture I want?" he asked, a sly look filling his face.

"On second thought, let me see," I commanded, motioning for the camera.

He moved closer and the scent of his aftershave filled my head. It was woodsy and made me wonder if he was one of those Bath and Body Works kinds of guys. The kind of guy who enjoyed rubbing lotion across his hard abs after a long day's work. *Liberty!* I yelled at myself. *Get a grip.* He did smell good, though. I couldn't deny that, even if I did need to control my thoughts.

He flipped through the pictures again for me and I was fascinated by them. He glanced at me. "What? Do you not like any of them?"

I shook my head and put my hand on his arm. "I was just thinking how cool it looks when you go through them that way. Like a video of me working, but in stills."

"That's the effect time-lapse gives. I love it because I never miss that perfect shot. A little nuance with their smile, or change in sunlight, that only the camera picks up with fast shutter action," he explained, punching the button forward a couple of times. "If it were me making the choice, I would use one of these two."

He showed me them again and I looked closely. I was surprised to see myself like that. It was a close up of me, intent on my work with my hair spilling around my shoulders. The sunlight framed the back of the window and the words *Liberty Belle* were nicely highlighted to the right of me.

"You do good work, Bram. I know I give you a hard time, but these are really good. You can use either of those for the paper," I answered and he nodded, saving them to the roll.

"If you give me your email, I'll send you all of them. Then you can use them as you see fit. I'll also send a release with them in case you want them printed." He flipped open his notepad and I wondered how many other women's emails were in there. I sighed and shook my head to clear my thoughts.

"That would be great. It's time to get some new rack cards printed for the tourists. You can send the pictures to hellsbells@gmail.com." I spelled it for him and his hand hesitated on the .com.

"Hells bells? That's hilarious, Liberty," he

laughed, tucking the notebook away.

"My dad always said that when I got in trouble. *Hells bells, girl, what were you thinking?* It's a way to never forget him," I explained quietly.

He glanced around the room and then met my eyes again. "I would think coming here every day would keep that from happening."

"In a professional way, yes, but not in the personal way that made him my dad."

"You still live in the house you grew up in..." he said slowly.

"It's true, I do. The thing is, he's not there anymore. Other than his old recliner, there's nothing left to remind me of him. His memory has faded almost as much as my mom's has, and that scares me. I hold onto the little things I have left so I can keep them in my heart." I motioned at the notebook and shrugged. "I don't know if that makes sense to anyone but me, but that's how I feel."

He rubbed my arm in a way that said he cared. "How long has he been gone now?"

I tried not to focus on his hand rubbing my arm and took a deep breath. "Three years today, actually. Sometimes, it feels like just yesterday, and sometimes it feels like forever ago."

Before I knew what was happening, he had his arms around me, his chest warm through the thin cotton of my work shirt.

"I'm sorry, Liberty. That's a tough anniversary, I'm sure. They both loved you so much," he whispered against my ear.

I fought at the tears that sprung to my eyes but didn't fight against hugging him back. Sometimes it felt good to hug someone, even if that someone was a Catholic schoolboy controlled by the devil.

He pulled back and smiled at me, but I glanced down and away, self-conscious of my own tears. I cleared my throat. "Thanks for coming in, Bram. I should close up and go home. I need a nap."

"Sure, no problem, Liberty. I'll get out of your hair and head back to the paper. I'll email you later. Get some rest."

He pulled the door open and the bell tinkled, making me look up out of habit. I turned the lock over as he walked past the window and slid his shades into place. He raised his hand in a wave and I raised mine back, unsure why it was shaking.

Chapter Three

Bram

"Thanks for helping me with this, Dully," I said again as I sanded down the wood after I cut it with the chop saw.

Dully was leaning back on a stool, taking a drink from a longneck bottle. He looked tired, and probably would rather be in the house sleeping than out here with me.

"It's no problem, Bram. A six-pack of beer and my little brother doesn't make for a bad Saturday night," he assured me, but I still felt a little guilty.

"You look tired. Is Jo-Jo still not sleeping?" I asked while he held the two boards together so I could screw them in place.

When I put the drill down, he answered, "She's doing okay for being only a month old. I'm the one not sleeping well, to be honest."

I sat back on my own stool and took a drag from my bottle. "How come? Is Snow okay?"

He ran his hands through his sandy brown hair. It was the exact same color and cut as mine, but he was twice my size, and a lot older. "Snow is good, Sunny is good, Jo-Jo is good and things should be good, but they're not. Work isn't good, that's the problem," he answered as I went back to the project.

"Work? Is the school having financial problems again?"

He shook his head. "No, the district is fine financially. This is about a student."

"Oh, I'm sorry. I know you sometimes struggle with that stuff, but you can't really talk about it."

He sighed heavily and nodded. "It's the part they don't tell you about in college when they teach you how to teach. I wish I had a way to turn that off in my mind, but I can't figure out how. I should be used to the ups and downs of special needs kids. I grew up with one," he explained, frustration obvious on his face.

I sanded at a rough spot a little bit before I glanced up. "It's true, we did, but the responsibility of Jay didn't fall on our shoulders, it fell on Mom and Dad's. Maybe it would help if you look at it as the responsibility of their education partly falls on you, but not their whole life. That falls on their mom and dad," I suggested, going back to my measuring.

"That is how I look at it, except in this case, the student doesn't have either. It's killing me to come home to my sweet little family and he's going home to nothing," Dully answered, rubbing his hands on his thighs repeatedly.

"Dully, I'm sorry. I didn't know," I apologized sincerely. "Is there anything we can do to help?"

He shook his head and took another beer from the cardboard carrier, swigging it down in one pull.

I grasped his shoulder and held his gaze. "Dully, slow it down. I need your help and we're working with power tools. Snow would have my head if you got hurt." I tried to joke a little and he looked up, almost as though he forgot what we were doing.

"Yeah, sorry, of course. Why are we building steps again?" he asked before he grabbed another board off the sawhorse and measured it against mine.

"Because I don't want Liberty to get hurt," I answered, then turned the saw on to drown out his questions.

It didn't work. As soon as it was quiet again, he kept up his questions. "She needs steps at the bakery door or what? I'm confused." He picked up the board from the saw and carried it to the workbench.

"You know how short she is," I paused and he nodded, "well, the other day when I went in to get Jo-Jo's cake, she tried to get up on a stool to see over the case, but she fell," I told him again, knowing I had told him all this before. He really was out of sorts, that much was certain.

"Oh, right, and you helped her up and noticed she was using an old stool without steps," he snapped his fingers, remembering the story from Sunday.

"Yeah, it's not safe. I also noticed that she's wearing a brace on her right leg." I dropped that nugget of information and then turned the drill on to screw the last two pieces of wood into place.

"Like a knee brace? Did she hurt herself?" he asked, grabbing the sander.

I paused and leaned against the counter. "Not a knee brace, no. It's like one of those braces that Snow has, but never wears, what are they called?"

"A KAFO. A knee, ankle and foot orthotic. If that's the case, then she didn't just hurt herself, something is really wrong. Did she say anything?"

"No, and I didn't let on that I noticed. Something told me she wouldn't appreciate it."

"You think? She's nothing but fire that girl. I think it's how she has survived the past five years with any sense of sanity. She's gone through so much, and now I'm even more worried about her," he admitted, turning the sander on and smoothing down the small set of steps we had just finished.

When I left the bakery last Sunday with the cake, I sent a text to a couple guys who hooked me up with a set of plans and some wood. At the baptism, I talked Dully into helping me in Dad's woodshop. They were a simple set of stairs, but they would keep her safe. Dully flicked the sander off and turned them each way, checking for rough patches.

I held the other side when he flipped them over. "Yesterday was the anniversary of her dad's death. She was really down when I stopped in to get a new picture for the summer insert. It must be hard going to work there every day with what happened. I know I couldn't do it if it was our dad," I admitted frankly, not ashamed to say it.

"It might seem that way to us, but for her, it's probably comforting because the bakery was his life, besides her and her mom. The bakery was his legacy to her, so when she's in that space, she feels them around her."

I shrugged. "I guess maybe." I picked up the stairs and set them on end, on the floor. "Thanks for helping me with them. You know my skill level isn't much above building a square box. They turned out great."

He sat back on the stool and took another beer. "I'm happy to help. I just hope you aren't getting in so deep you can't get out."

I set my beer bottle down hard. "And what does that mean?"

"It means I know you had a thing for her in high school and she refused to go out with you. I hope you aren't still carrying that old flame."

"I didn't have a thing for her in high school, and so what if I did. What if I am carrying a flame for her? That's my business, not yours," I said angrily. "I'm trying to be a good friend and keep her from getting hurt because I care about her, and she's got no one. Is that such a bad thing? I thought that's what we did in Snowberry. I thought we helped each other out."

I stood and picked up the steps. "Thanks for

the help. Talk to you later," I grumbled, headed straight for my SUV. I pulled open the back hatch and threw the wooden stairs in, my hand reaching for the handle to pull it back down.

His hand was holding it open, so I couldn't slam it the way I wanted to. "I never said it was a bad thing, Bram. I just don't want to see you get hurt because you have feelings for her, and she can't reciprocate. She's been hurt a lot in her short life."

He let go of the hatch and I pulled it down, making sure it latched. "I get it, Dully. I'm not one of your students. Tell Snow hi for me, and kiss the girls."

I slid into the seat and put the SUV in reverse, trying not to feel like a jerk when my headlights swept across his face and showed me how much I had hurt him.

Liberty

I glanced up from the bench when I thought I heard knocking on the back door. I checked my watch, but it wasn't even six a.m., and on a Sunday to boot. There wasn't a soul who should be knocking on my door. Unless it was Noel picking up the pies, but it was even too early for him.

I went to the door. "Who is it?"

"It's Bram Alexander," came the voice from the other side.

I sighed and pulled it open. "Good morning, Bram. I'm not open yet."

He motioned at the door. "I know, that's why I knocked."

He winked at me and I tried not to let his ridiculously cute face make me do something I would regret, like let him in the door, literally and figuratively. "Oh, I got the pictures the other day. I think I sent a return thank you, didn't I?"

He nodded. "Yup, you did. I'm glad the old interwebs did its job."

"Perfect, well, have a good Sunday." I smiled congenially while I pushed the door closed.

He reached out with his foot and blocked it. "I'm not here about the pictures. I brought you something, but didn't want to bring it in during customer hours."

I pulled the door open wider. "You brought me something?"

"Yeah," he said quietly and picked up whatever he had leaned against the building. It was too dark to see and I motioned him in, closing the door behind him.

He held a set of wooden stairs in his hand and braced them against the floor. "Dully and I made these steps for the bakery case. That stool isn't safe," he explained, pointing toward the front.

"You made me steps?" I asked, not at all happy to hear my voice give away how shocked I was.

"Was that out of line? I just thought they would be safer than the stool, but you don't have to use them." He was backpedaling toward the door and I reached for him.

I shook my head when he stopped. "No, it wasn't at all out of line. I'm just surprised. Thank you, Bram."

The thank you was sincere because I was touched that he cared that much about me.

He grinned and picked them up, carrying them to the front of the bakery. He moved behind the cases and handed me the old wooden box I usually use.

"Dully and I figured they would stay sound on the rubber mats, but we added some extra grip to the bottom just to be sure." He set the stairs on end and pulled out several longer pieces of wood, and then laid the stairs down in front of the case. "Is that a good spot?" he asked, and I nodded, the lump in my throat stopping any words from coming out.

He turned back to the stairs and fixed the longer pieces of wood along the edges, so there was a handrail on each side. "Go ahead, try them." He motioned for me to climb up them, so I did, working to make sure my legs moved equally, even though I knew from his angle, they didn't.

I went up and down them a couple times and then stood next to them. "No one has ever done anything this nice for me before," I said, trying not to cry.

He leaned on the handrail a little and brushed my hand with his. "I just didn't want you to get hurt. This concrete floor could do a lot of damage if you fall on it wrong."

"Is your night job rescuing damsels in distress?" I asked half-jokingly, trying to hide my emotions.

He cocked his head. "What do you mean?"

"First, April, and now me," I said and his eyes held surprise. "I know about April. She works for Noel, you know."

He worked his hand around like an artist's brush. "Oh, that, no big deal. Dully and I are volunteer firefighters, we're trained for that."

"You're trained to shimmy out on thin ice, tied to nothing but your brother by a rope, to save a drowning woman?" I asked and he nodded, bouncing on his toes a little. I noticed he did that when he was nervous.

"Yup," he answered, and I raised a brow.

"Did they also train you in building stairs for short girls in bakeries?" I teased and he shook his head.

"No, that required a six-pack of beer and Dully's help. I'm not great at woodworking, but we managed."

He smiled and I felt warm under his gaze. It was the way I used to feel every time he would come in and order a Bavarian cream bear claw the first few years after my father died. I hadn't seen him much over the last year, and having him in the bakery again was unsettling, yet comforting.

I cleared my throat. "You more than managed, you really helped me out. I appreciate it, Bram. Things have been hard lately and …" I motioned at the stairs, my throat thick again, so I couldn't finish the sentence.

"Come here," he whispered, giving me a hug. It was short and gentle, but caring and supportive at the same time. "Sometimes, we just need a little help from our friends."

I nodded, not making eye contact. "I'm not great at asking for help, so thank you. You've saved the day. I planned to order a set, but I couldn't find anything even close to what I needed. I want to pay you for them," I said suddenly.

"No, peace of mind in knowing your safe is payment enough, Liberty," he insisted, walking around the corner to the workbench.

I grabbed his jacket to stop him. "At least let me pay you for the materials. I know that wasn't cheap."

He turned to me slowly, his eyes coming to rest on mine. "You know how you can pay me?" I shook my head no and he picked up my hand. "Come have a drink with me tonight. I'll even let you buy."

I laughed and glanced up at the ceiling. "You Alexander boys. You always have an angle."

"I'm not angling, not at all. I just like your company and that's the only payment I'll accept," he said, crossing his arms.

I held my hands up in surrender. "Okay, fine, I'll

go for a drink with you. I close at one on Sunday and then I'll need a nap. I've been up since three."

He smiled as if he just won the lottery, and I almost rethought the decision. "That's perfect. When I finish dinner at Mom and Dad's, I'll pick you up. Say seven?"

"Seven sounds great, Bram," I conceded. "Do me a favor?"

"Sure, anything," he agreed.

I gathered a pie, rolls, cookies, and a dozen donuts, and packaged them up then handed them to him. "Take the pie and rolls to your mom for dinner, the cookies to Sunny, and the donuts to Dully. Tell them I appreciate them, please."

He grinned around his heavily laden arms, resting his chin on the top of the pie container. "They love this kind of thanks."

"Oh!" I exclaimed, "Hang tight, I forgot one thing." I went to the rack by the oven and pulled down a pan. It was covered in steaming hot bear claws. I took a plastic donut container and laid several in the bottom, snapping the lid closed. "You haven't been in for Bavarian cream bear claws in a long time. I make them every day, just in case you happen to stop by. Looks like today it finally paid off."

I set the container of pastry on top of the pie and it was at eye level for him. He peeked above the container and straight into my soul. "Looks like today was my lucky day in more ways than one. See you at seven," he said while I held the door open.

"See you at seven, Bram."

He turned back to me when he got to his car. "For the record, being without your sweets the last year has made it one of the most boring, and empty, years of my life. I'm giving you fair warning, once I taste your sweetness on my tongue again, I won't be able to stay away."

Chapter Four

Bram

"You're missing out on the pie," Dully's voice said from behind me and I turned, resting my back on the rail of the deck.

"I'm already full from dinner," I answered.

Dully sat down on the bench and watched the sunlight waning in the sky, but didn't say anything more.

"Listen, Dully, I'm sorry about being a jerk last night. I know what you were trying to say, and I appreciate that you're always looking out for me," I told him, sitting next to him on the bench.

"It's forgotten, Bram. How did she like the stairs?" he asked, staring down at his hands.

"She cried, actually. Said no one has ever done anything that nice for her. She asked me to tell you how much she appreciates that you helped me get them done. She wanted to pay me, but I refused, so she sent baked goods instead," I joked, and he laughed without glancing up.

"Liberty's pie is payment enough. I'm glad she liked them and she'll be safer now," he said, clasping his hands in front of him.

"She agreed to go for a drink with me tonight. I'm picking her up at seven. Don't worry, we're just going as friends. I can tell she needs one, that's all."

"I never said you couldn't be more than friends, Bram. I just said to be careful," he answered in kind.

I rested my hand on his shoulder. "Dully, are you okay? I've never seen you this down before."

He rocked a little on the bench as though that was supposed to be him nodding. He swiped at his nose and I realized my big brother was crying. "Dully, my God, what's going on?" I asked and dropped to one knee next to him.

He rested his head in his palm and closed his eyes. "I think I'm having a mental breakdown or something," he tried to joke. "I can't get this student out of my mind, or my heart, and it's killing me slowly. I can't sleep, and I can't even look at my babies without wanting to cry. I come to Sunday dinner and look around the table at my wonderful family, and I can't stop the tears. All I can think about is how sad he must be right now. I don't know why this is happening to me. I've never been this way with my students before."

"Have you talked to Snow? She's pretty good at helping me sort myself out when I need it."

"No, she has so much to worry about as it is," he sighed.

I kept my hand on his shoulder and glanced up, catching Snow watching us. I motioned for her to come out and she had her wheelchair moving instantly.

"I think you need to talk to her about it, bro. You're supposed to be partners," I encouraged as the patio door slid open and Snow rolled out.

Dully glanced up and saw her, quickly swiping at his face as though she wouldn't see his pain. She rolled next to him and put her arms around his back. "I'm fine," he promised, but she just laughed and shook her head.

"No, you're not. I'm not so tired I haven't noticed what's going on. I've been waiting for you to talk to me about it, but for some reason, you can't find a way. Mom is watching the girls until Lila Jo wakes up and needs to eat. Let's go home and talk. You have to tell me what's going on. Maybe I can help," she whispered.

He reached over and hugged the thin woman in the wheelchair, my heart aching at the pain my big, strong brother was struggling to explain. I stood up and brushed off my jeans. She held her hand out and I took it for a moment until she smiled up at me and gave me a wink. I stepped through the patio door and slid it closed, confident she would help him sort out his feelings.

I watched them cross the path toward their house until they disappeared among the trees. The two of them reminded me of the old saying, *sometimes love hurts*.

Something told me that was an idea I had better get used to.

Liberty

I gazed at the man who sat across from me. His red, white, and blue button-up shirt was rolled casually at the elbows, and he sported a white t-shirt under it. He was leaning back in his chair, trying to look relaxed, but the way he was spinning his beer bottle told me he was anything but. When he arrived at my house, he had a single yellow rose in his hand and a smile on his face, but that looked forced, too. I guess now is as good as time as any to sort out his discord.

"So, how did Sunday dinner go?" I asked, sipping my white wine. It wasn't smart to go with anything stronger when I had to be up at three a.m.

"Great, yeah, really good. Everyone loved your pie. Mom said to tell you thank you, and she'll be by for coffee later this week." He smiled and took a sip of his beer.

"Good, I love it when your mom stops by for coffee. I always take a break and visit with her. She makes me feel like a daughter again. It's been a while since I've been one of those."

He sat forward. "You're still her daughter, even if your mom's not here with you anymore."

I held my hand up to clarify. "I know, I just meant that sometimes I feel like an orphan. I'm only twenty-five and my whole family is dead. The only person who resembles family at all is my best friend, but she goes to college and the only time I see her is when she comes in to work a shift. Your mom makes me feel loved. That's all I meant."

He leaned back again with understanding. "She's good at that, making someone feel loved. I'm sorry you lost your parents so early in life. I can't even begin to understand how you feel."

It was as though whatever he was upset about was somehow tied to the words he just said. He turned away from me and toward the bar, swirling his finger around his head for another round. When he picked me up, we decided we would go to the only half-decent bar in town. The atmosphere was upscale, and they served simple food along with their drinks. He was quiet again until the barmaid brought another round. I glanced up and smiled at a girl I went to school with.

"Hey, Fiona, I think we need an appetizer. What do you recommend?" I asked.

She held the tray in front of her with an order pad on it, her pen tapping a bit while she thought about the choices. "We have a great artichoke dip made with fresh Wisconsin mozzarella and served with an outstanding French bread from this little bakery in town." She grinned and Bram chuckled, but I didn't make eye contact with him.

"That sounds perfect, thanks."

She tucked the tray under her arm, "Great, give us a few minutes and I'll bring it out." She disappeared back behind the bar and I took a sip of my wine.

"Tell me what's really bothering you, Bram. Or am I boring you?" I asked straight up, hoping to catch him off guard.

He almost choked on his swallow of beer. "No, of course not. Everything is fine," he assured me, but I just lifted one brow.

"We've been here for twenty minutes and you've said about six sentences. Usually, you talk nonstop, so something is definitely wrong," I said, watching him closely.

"I'm worried about Dully. Last night when we were working on the steps, he told me he's not sleeping because he's always worrying about this orphan in his class. Tonight, I was talking to him on the deck at Mom and Dad's, and he started crying …" he trailed off and shrugged, probably afraid to say too much and embarrass Dully.

I reached over and took his hand. "Wow, that's two people in one day that you made cry. It's a record," I teased, but he didn't look amused. "I'm not trying to make light of the situation, Bram. I agree that's very out of character for Dully."

He shrugged again and brought the beer bottle to his lips. "When I left, Mom was going to watch the babies so he and Snow could talk. Apparently, he hasn't even told her about it. He tries to carry all this around inside and never lets on when something is bothering him. I know he's trying not to worry Snow, but it's having the opposite effect.

She's worried sick. I hope they work it out."

Fiona walked toward us, carrying the dip and sliced bread. I made room on the table for the plate and the break in the conversation was a good way to lighten the mood and move on.

"Thanks, Fiona, it smells heavenly," I told her, taking one of the small plates from her hand.

"Enjoy, and let me know if you need anything else." She waved before heading back to the bar.

"Aren't you going to have some?" I asked, dishing up some dip and bread on my plate. I had to negate the effects of the alcohol in my system, so I didn't fall down when I stood up. My right hand was shaking as I scooped, I noticed, so I tucked it under the table and ate with my left hand.

"I was just waiting for you to get yours." He smiled at me and it looked more natural as he took a plate and helped himself.

We ate in silence for a few moments while he blatantly ogled me over the rim of his beer bottle. I couldn't say he had changed much since high school. He was always a straight forward, tell it like it is, kind of guy. He didn't mix words and he didn't pretend to be someone he wasn't.

While Dully was playing every sport on the docket, Bram was in the yearbook and photography club. Instead of going off to college for a degree after high school, he worked with a renowned photographer in the Twin Cities for a year, and then came back to Snowberry to work at the paper. His side business of wedding photography was taking off and he was always on the go. He had a skilled eye for the human element.

"Do you think growing up with Jay is the reason you see things through the lens like you do?" I asked between bites.

He lowered his bread to his plate. "Excuse me?"

"I mean because of the way you put people at ease when you take pictures of them. You find their best feature and bring that out. Like the pictures of me, for instance, you found that the best feature was the cake and you really went for it." I grinned and he started to choke on his bread. He coughed quietly, trying not to cause a scene for the rest of the bar.

"Girl, I wasn't taking pictures of the cake," he laughed quietly. "I was taking pictures of fabulous you. The dang thing just kept getting in the frame."

"Imagine that," I joked, ignoring his use of fabulous as a descriptor for me.

"Oh, you don't believe me?" He grabbed his phone out of his pocket and opened it up. He came over to me and held the camera out above us, "Say selfie," he commanded again and hit the button. He caught me with my tongue sticking out and my hand half-covering my face.

He laughed hysterically, then sat back down and took a drink from his beer bottle. "I guess we will have to keep working on that skill, but I get what you're asking, and I guess in a way it probably did. Dully and Jay are super close. I think it's just the way Dully is made up. He wants to be the protector, and since I didn't need one, he chose Jay." He shrugged, and whatever look was on my face left him flustered enough he started to rub his forehead. "I mean, we all have a great relationship, but I didn't let Jay's issues dictate my life as much as Dully did. I think because he was older, he wanted to take some of the burden off Mom and Dad. That said, you don't grow up spending time at children's hospitals and at Paralympics and not have that change how you see life."

I leaned back a little to put him at ease. "I remember in high school you always took the best pictures for the yearbook. You once took a picture of my friend who always thought she was ugly and fat, but when she saw the picture, she felt like the prom queen. You changed how she looked at herself with just one picture that day," I told him and he stared hard at me for sincerity.

"Really? I had no idea. Thank you for sharing that with me."

"It takes real talent to do what you do. You're going somewhere with your photography, and I admire your determination to follow your heart. Snow and Dully must love having a family photographer for the girls. In a way, you will be documenting their lives together."

He laughed his genuine laugh then. The one that always made me do an involuntary shiver imagining what it would feel like against my chest.

He nodded as though I just told the best joke in

the whole world. "I take way too many pictures of those babies, but Sunny is always doing something adorable. It's hard not to be snapping selfies with her. I take her with me to the Paralympics sometimes, if Jay is competing, and she's always a good helper."

"Oh, you take pictures for Jay?" I asked, and he waved his hand in front of his plate as he swallowed his bread.

"Not just for Jay. I'm the official Paralympics photographer, or rather I was before I resigned the end of last year. It's too hard with the competitions on Saturday and weddings also on Saturday. I've done it for a lot of years and it was time to let someone else have the opportunity."

I leaned toward him again. "I didn't know there was such a thing as an official photographer, but I guess it makes sense. I bet you got some really cool action shots."

"Oh, yeah, some of the chairs out there nowadays are like finely-tuned machines. Jay is playing wheelchair basketball in Sport and that chair licks them all, though. You know that Snow built Sport for him, right?"

I nodded. "It's pretty much like hers with the voice recognition technology, only made for sports, from what I understand."

"Right, she made his chair to be an everyday chair, but also to be used for sports. Snow has a brilliant mind. She scares me she's so smart."

I held my hand up in solidarity. "I hear you.

She definitely intimidates me even as small as she is, but then she goes and does something so sweet you can't help but see her as a friend."

"You're totally right there, she's good at putting people at ease. I think that's because she senses how people feel inferior to her intelligence, even though she says we shouldn't *because she's not that smart*." He stopped and rolled his eyes at her favorite line. "I remember the first time Dully brought her to dinner. I was totally standoffish, you know, not even having a college degree, and it was like she zeroed in on me and wouldn't let go until I opened up."

I pointed my finger at him. "And that's how come you know Dully will be just fine once he talks to her. She will help him sort out how he's feeling and work with him to find a solution to what's bothering him," I finished and he gave me one firm nod.

"Exactly. To be honest, I thought that growing up in the Alexander family really changed how I saw life from the way other kids saw it. But now that I'm grown, the family is still changing how I see life. I have a sister-in-law in a wheelchair and a brother in a wheelchair who has a new wife. I have a good friend who is deaf and, by the way, I can't wait to do the pictures next week for that wedding, and last year I did the wedding photos for a woman who was in terrible pain, but still looked drop-dead gorgeous on her big day. I don't know, sometimes I think I'm snapping these photos for a reason," he admitted, shrugging one shoulder haphazardly.

"The doctors think I have MS," I blurted out and then froze in place.

Did I just say that?

The look on his face told me I had.

I stood up in a flash and nearly tipped over, but righted myself in time. I grabbed my coat off the chair in a jerky motion. "I have to go," I cried, and headed straight for the door as fast as the leg brace would allow.

Chapter Five

"Liberty!" he called from somewhere behind me in the dark. "Dammit, Liberty, wait!"

I kept walking, even though I knew the leg brace would slow me down and Bram would catch me before I got home. Tears burned in the back of my eyes and my throat felt like it was going to explode. Why did I have to go and ruin our fun time together?

That wasn't need-to-know information, Liberty. You should have kept your mouth shut.

His hand grasped my arm and I tried to shake it off, but he wasn't having any part of it. "Liberty, stop, please."

"I have to go home," I said quietly, my steps never slowing. I was only a block away and could see the glow of my front porch light from the sidewalk.

I thought about all the times I used to come home late from basketball games. I would find that light shining in the darkness, and my parents in their pajamas watching The Late Show while they waited up for me. It was a good feeling that I tried to zero in on. His presence next to me was making it hard to do, though. I refused to make eye contact, and by the time I got to my street, I was exhausted. I couldn't take long walks anymore, and that was just another frustrating part of the disease.

He was still following me, and I was distracted when I stepped down off the curb. Not thinking, I went down with my right leg, which promptly gave out, and I fell into the street, landing on my hands in the gravel. His hands had my waist, but the damage was already done.

"Why are you so damn stubborn?" he asked while he helped me stand up and checked my hands. They were bleeding and had little pieces of gravel in them.

He half-walked, half-carried me to my front door since my leg wasn't going to finish the short distance to the house. "Where are your keys?" he asked and I moaned.

"I forgot my purse at the bar." I sighed, the sound coming out more like a sob.

"This purse?" he asked and held it up. I nodded then dropped my chin to my chest.

"Keys are in the front," I whispered.

He dug them out and opened the door for me. I was never more grateful to be home, and I collapsed on the couch for a minute, still holding my hands out in front of me.

He set my purse down on the table and came over, helping me up with an arm around my waist. In the bathroom, he held me up while he ran cool water over my hands to clean them. Once they were dry, he applied some ointment and a Band-Aid to each, and then took me back to the couch.

I couldn't look at him. I couldn't handle him being in my living room, knowing my secret. I may have turned him down for every other date he's ever asked me on, but that wasn't because I wanted to. I turned him down because I was afraid. Afraid if I went out with him, I would end up falling for him. Afraid if we became more than friends, he would leave me someday, too.

"Tonight was a bad idea. I'm not the best company right now. I didn't mean to ruin the evening," I apologized, and he sat down on the coffee table in front of the couch.

"I don't remember saying you were bad company. I also don't remember saying you ruined the evening," he pointed out.

I rested my head back on the couch. "I didn't pay the bill. I need to call them."

"I took care of it, Liberty. We're square," he assured me, and I struggled to sit up on the big cushy couch.

"Let me give you the money. It was supposed to be my treat." I pointed at my purse, but he didn't reach for it. Instead, he reached for me.

His hand touched my leg and he looked me straight in the eye. "Liberty, why are you being like this?"

"Like what? I said I would pay, and I'll pay," I grumbled, my voice shaking when I spoke. That meant the exhaustion had taken hold, and I wasn't going to move off this couch until morning.

"I don't want your money. I want to know why you think you had to run out of there because you told me something personal. Is it that hard for you to share things about yourself?"

I forced myself to look up into his face. His eyes were sincere as they stared me down, his gaze intent on my face.

Was it hard for me to share things about myself? That's the understatement of the century, pal.

"I don't know why I said that. I really shouldn't have, and I apologize for being a downer," I answered instead.

He took me by the shoulders and shook me a little. "Stop it. Just stop acting as though you're fine when all evidence leads to the contrary. You can't walk around pretending like this isn't happening if it is, Liberty."

"If I do that, pretend like it isn't happening, then I can keep going. If I admit that it is, I'll fall apart, Bram. I don't have time to fall apart," I tried to explain with my voice full of tears. "I don't have the time, or energy, to face reality right now."

"I think it's more that you don't have any emotional support to help you face reality," he said gently.

I couldn't stop the tears now that they started, so I laid my head back on the couch and closed my eyes. I heard him get up and go into my kitchen. The kitchen I used to share with my mom and dad.

He ran the faucet my mom used to fill her soup pot, and he opened the cupboard where my dad used to keep his favorite mug. I cried silently, hating that when I finally fell apart, *he* was the one to witness it.

I heard his movements as he made tea and carried it over, setting it on the table. The couch dipped when he sat down next to me, and then he laid his hand over mine. Every so often, he reached up and wiped away a tear with his thumb.

"God, I'm sorry for falling apart like this," I whispered, taking a drink of the tea.

"You really need to stop apologizing, Liberty. If I didn't want to be here, I wouldn't be," he scolded.

I nodded, leaning back again. Before I could touch the back of the couch, he had me against his chest. He smoothed his hand across my back as though he did it all the time. The strange part was, it felt comforting and natural, almost like we should do it all the time.

Check yourself back into reality, Liberty. Bram Alexander isn't interested in a lifelong relationship with you.

"I'm sure you noticed the brace on my leg," I sighed, resigned to having the conversation with him I didn't want to have.

"I'm observant like that," he agreed.

"I would have to fall right in front of a newspaperman," I lamented, and he chuckled, squeezing me tighter. "It was Easter time when my right leg suddenly became unexplainably weak. I thought I had hurt it at first and tried to baby it, but it just kept getting worse. I was falling all the time and finally didn't have a choice but to go to the doctor. He ordered the brace, which helps, but sometimes I have to use a cane when I get really tired or I'll fall down."

"What do the doctors think the weakness is from?" he asked. "Is that why they brought up the MS?"

I scrubbed my hand down over my face. "Muscle weakness is classic for multiple sclerosis, Bram. I'm sure you also noticed my hand shaking doing simple things that shouldn't take any effort."

"I just thought you had too much alcohol," he bantered and that got him a laugh.

"I wish. Unfortunately, not the case. Add that to the fatigue I've had lately, and the doctors are concerned."

"You get up very early and work hard, maybe that's why you're tired."

"I'm twenty-five and I get plenty of sleep. It's more like exhaustion I can't shake unless I nap in the afternoon. Up until a few months ago, I never had that, and my schedule hasn't changed." I sipped the tea and the simple act of holding the cup made my hand shake.

He noticed and took it from my hand. "Okay, that's probably not normal for someone our age. What are they going to do?"

"I have to have an MRI this week, and they will

look for areas in my brain that suggest MS plaques. I think clinically they have already decided, considering my mother's history."

"Your mother?" he asked slowly, and I sighed, rubbing my hand over my face again.

"My mother had MS, Bram. She had it for twenty years before she died."

The words were barely out of my mouth and he made a sound like he had been punched in the gut. "I had no idea, Liberty. She was always so much bigger than life when I was a kid. Is that ..." he stopped, and I stared up at him. I saw the question on his face.

"Is that what caused the accident?" I asked and he nodded. "We don't know what caused it. She wasn't in a relapsed state when the accident happened, so the doctors don't think so, but being one hundred percent sure isn't possible."

"I thought only older people got MS. Is it hereditary?"

I shook my head. "Surprisingly, a lot of younger people are diagnosed with it, even some kids. The researchers don't believe it is hereditary, but they know if you have a family member with it, you have a higher chance of having it, too. They think there is a gene that, if triggered by an environmental factor, the MS will develop. In my mom's case, and probably mine, it could have been something that we used in the bakery, but there is no way to know for sure."

"I see," he whispered. "It has to be hard to have

so many unanswered questions."

I nodded, laughing sadly. "Incredibly hard. I'm scared they will tell me I have MS, but then I'm scared they will tell me I don't have it, and they don't know what's causing this."

"The enemy you know versus the one you don't," he pondered. "When do you go for the tests?"

"I have the MRI Wednesday afternoon and see the doctor on Friday. I'm going to have Lucinda work the weekend shifts in the front. That way, if I'm a mess, I can stay in the back, and go home when I'm done baking," I reasoned.

"What can I do to help?" he asked, rubbing my arm.

I sighed and shook my head. "As much as I hate to admit it, you're helping me right now. I haven't told anyone but Lucinda about this and it's been building up inside me. I'm scared, Bram, and I don't have anyone to talk to about it."

"That's understandable, Liberty. I'm glad I can be your friend tonight, and that you trust me enough to tell me how you're feeling. I promise this will stay between us until you say otherwise," he said, laying a kiss on my forehead.

The feel of his lips on my skin made me relax into his chest. As much as I was scared to be in his arms, I trusted that my secret was safe with him.

Chapter Six

Bram

I woke up slowly. The weight on my chest and hip, reminding me I wasn't in my bed at home. I gazed down at the blonde-haired beauty asleep on my chest. My heart constricted when I thought about what she has dealt with in her life. I've gone through enough *this sucks* situations in my own life, but she's had more than her fair share.

She's twenty-five and trying to run a business while sick, now that sucks. She's twenty-five with no family or support, and that sucks the most. No one deserves to go through what she is going through alone. I should break my promise and tell my Mom, and Snow about it. She might get upset with me, but I know she will need someone to lean on. It's a chance I'll have to take. There are so many people in Snowberry who would hold her up, physically and emotionally, if they knew what she was dealing with, but she will never tell them. Liberty reminds me a little of Dully in that she always tries to act as though she's fine when she's not.

I glanced at my watch and saw it was nearly three a.m. I knew she had to get back to the bakery and I shook her gently. "Liberty, you gotta wake up sweetheart, it's time to make the donuts."

She sat straight up as though she just had the worst nightmare of her life. I had to hang on to her waist, so she didn't try to stand.

"Shhh, it's okay. You just fell asleep. I didn't want you to miss your morning orders, though," I whispered, not sure why since no one else was in the house.

"I fell asleep on you?" she asked.

I laughed a little while I stroked her spine gently to lessen the tension in her back. "Yeah, and I promptly fell asleep, too, so don't feel bad. Let me get you to work and then I'll head home." I stood and helped her stand up. I could tell she was stiff, and her leg didn't want to move the way it should. Falling asleep with the brace on was probably not going to help later today. Her blouse had fallen to the side, revealing the soft white flesh of her left breast. I wanted to reach out and feel her skin under mine. I wanted to ... I swallowed against the need in the pit of my stomach.

She needs a friend, not a creep, Bram.

"I'm not sure I can walk without fixing this brace first. It's all twisted," she said, sitting back down. She glanced up at me expectantly and I waited for her to take it off. "Umm, I have to take my pants off to get at the brace. It goes around my waist."

"Oh right, sorry, I knew that. I'll use the bathroom." I pointed toward the other room and she nodded. I closed the door behind me and leaned against it, banging my head on it a couple of times out of frustration. I was sure of one thing; those sad blue eyes were going to be my downfall if I wasn't careful with my heart.

Liberty

"Hey, Liberty, I'm here!" Lucinda called from the front.

I stood up from the computer where I was doing inventory and stretched. "Hey, Lucinda. Thanks for covering the last couple of hours for me," I said, taking my own apron off and tossing it in the dirty laundry bag.

She tied on a clean apron and tucked her hair in a hairnet, then washed her hands. "Not a problem at all. My classes are always done at noon, so I don't mind coming in to help. Want me to take the deposit to the bank when I close?"

I tossed it around in my mind, wondering if I was going to feel like coming back after the test was over. Chances were good I would just want to go home.

"I would appreciate that. You can do the same thing you do on the weekends. Except I only start the weekdays with three hundred in cash instead of four," I explained.

"Got it. I'll drop it off and you can take care of the rest in the morning. What about day-olds? Want me to package them up?" she asked, holding her notebook at the ready.

"Yup, pretty much whatever is left in the shop at closing has to go. Package the case donuts and call the nursing home, they will pick them up right away. Offer them anything else we have, too. Whatever they don't take, I'll give to the church to use for Sunday service or group meetings," I told her, and she wrote it all down.

"My guess is the nursing home will take what you've got with no complaints." She winked and I laughed, nodding my head.

"I'm just glad I have someplace to send it all. Okay, I have to be on my way to my appointment. I would say call if you have a problem, but I won't be reachable."

She hugged me the way only a best friend can. "Maybe we should just close the place down, so I can go with you," she whispered.

I hugged her tighter and considered it for a long moment, but backed out of the hug slowly. "As much as I love you, and don't want to do this alone, I also don't want to come back here when I'm done. I know it sounds strange, but you're helping me more taking care of all of this. I don't want to start tomorrow out behind. If you come with me, you'll just sit there for hours while I'm in a tube."

The look on her face told me she agreed, even if

she didn't like it. "Okay, I'll stay here, but you call me as soon as you're done. Got it? Now, off with you, before I change my mind."

I gave her a quick hug and then grabbed my coat off the rack by the door to cover my grungy white shirt. I wished I had brought clean clothes to put on, which was silly because they were just going to make me wear a hospital gown anyway.

Hope they enjoy the scent of frosting, I thought as I pushed open the door.

Leaning against my car was a visitor I wasn't expecting, and unfortunately, didn't have time to talk with.

"Holding up my Camry, Mrs. Alexander?" I asked, laughing a little.

"More like it's holding me up. I spent the morning with Jo-Jo and Sunny. They wear me out," she said, but her smile told me she loved every minute of it.

"Jo-Jo?" I asked, surprised at the nickname for the baby.

She held her arms out. "Sunny started calling her that after some clown on a cartoon show. Somehow it stuck, and we all call her that now."

I beeped open the lock on the car as I approached. "Leave it to kids, right? I would love to stay and chat, but I have an appointment. Can I take a rain check?"

She pulled the door handle open and sat down in the passenger seat as I got to the driver's side. I opened my door and looked in at her. The look on her face told me she knew. I plunked down into the seat and put my purse in the back. "He told you, didn't he?" I asked. I couldn't look at her, so I stared straight ahead at the grey brick building.

She laid her hand on my arm tenderly. "He did. He admitted he was breaking his promise, but maybe it would be nice to have a mom with you, even if it's not your own."

My chin trembled and I nodded my head quickly, without looking at her. "They offered to give me sedation because the test is so long, but I said no since I didn't have anyone to drive me home."

She brushed some hair back from my face and leaned forward, so I had to make eye contact. "That's where you're wrong. There are plenty of people who would have driven you home if you had asked, my son included. Why don't you let me drive over to the hospital? I don't think you should be driving."

"Okay," I sighed and tried to climb back out of the car. The leg brace was stuck, and she had to help me out by pushing the seat all the way back. I finally made it into the passenger seat after a few moments and buckled my seatbelt. "Thank you, Mrs. Alexander. I've been worried about this for days. Not the test itself, but what it might show."

She turned to me after she pulled the seat forward. "How about if you call me Suzie, okay? And you don't need to thank me. I'm glad you told Bram about this. I would feel terrible knowing you went through it alone. I'm a mom of a child who has had way too many of these tests. I would never want anyone to go through that alone."

I clasped my hands in front of me and stared down at them. "All the same, Suzie, it means more to me than you'll ever know."

I rested my head on the window and she backed out of the spot then quietly drove me to the hospital.

Chapter Seven

There was a knock on my door and I stood, steadying myself with the cane I hated, even if it was fashionable with pink zebra stripes. When Suzie brought me home from the hospital, I had showered and put on a pair of lounge pants and a t-shirt, then promptly fell asleep. The sedation was great for making the test not feel like the nearly two-hour ordeal it was, but it left me groggy and out of sorts.

The knock came again and I growled at the door. "Hang on, I'm coming," I yelled, aggravated at the intrusion.

I looked through the peephole and groaned inwardly. I should have expected he would show up, and here I am in my pajamas. I pulled the door open and plastered on a smile.

"Hi, Bram," I said, keeping the screen door between us.

"Hi, Liberty." He smiled that smile of his and I felt my resolve to send him packing waver a little. "Mom thought someone should check on you, so I swung by when I left the paper."

I stared at the box in his hands. "Right after

you swung by Gallo's?" I asked and he laughed deeply.

"Okay, you got me. I swung by Gallo's first, hoping you would be hungry enough to share a pizza with me. I'm worried about you," he answered, the final words coming out as though he hated to admit it.

I pushed the screen door open and held it until he grabbed it with his elbow. I stepped back and he walked past me to set the pizza down on my small table. I turned to close the door and when I turned back, he was staring right at me. He took a moment to study my rumpled t-shirt and the cane in my hand.

"Come here," he said to me, his arms out, but I shook my head.

"I don't think that's a good idea. You said that the other night and look what happened," I joked, but he didn't laugh.

"Be that as it may, you look like you've had a hard day and could use a hug," he pushed back, coming over to where I leaned on my cane.

He took the cane and put his arm around my waist, letting me use him for balance as I walked back to the living room and sat in Dad's old recliner. He knelt in front of me and held my hands, his eyes locked with mine.

"I've been worried about you all day. I won't stay long, but I had to see you. Will you share some pizza with me?"

I could feel his concern as it coursed through

his body and that was enough to make me nod my head, even though I wasn't hungry. He smiled at the small victory and pushed himself up off the floor. He went to my kitchen and puttered around as though he'd lived here his whole life. It was disconcertingly comfortable and intensely scary, at the same time.

I knew the moment he opened the box to the pizza because the smell of cheese and tomato sauce filled the space. My mouth watered instantly. Gallo's is as much of a landmark in this community as my bakery is. I cut my teeth on their crust and went there for my first date.

He stood in front of me, holding a plate, his head cocked to the side. "Whatcha thinking about?"

I took the plate from him and laughed. "I was thinking about Gallo's and how many firsts I had there. My first piece of pizza, my first communion, my first date …"

"You went to Gallo's for your first communion?" he asked as he made himself comfortable on the couch.

"I know that sounds dumb, doesn't it? But I demanded that's where we go." I shook my head a little. "I was a real pain sometimes, but as an only child, I got away with it."

I picked at the piece of pizza on my plate. It was slathered in pepperoni and green olives, the cheese oozing over the edges. I wanted to be hungry, but I couldn't force it past my lips.

"Are you mad at me?" he asked, setting his plate on the coffee table.

I glanced up, unsure of what he meant. "About?"

"Telling my mom. I know I promised I would keep it between us, but she has a lot of experience with tests. I didn't want you to be alone," he explained.

I stared down at my plate. "I'm not mad, and I didn't want to be alone, but I didn't have a lot of choice. Well, your mom says I did, but I didn't think so. She told me that you told her I needed a mom," I whispered, setting my plate on the stand next to me.

He scratched his head. "Yeah, hearing it from your lips, it comes off sounding not quite how I meant it. I know you have a mom. I just meant that maybe you could use some comfort from another mom."

"I know how you meant it, and you were right. I definitely needed a mom today. I was really glad to see her leaning against my car when I opened the door," I shared honestly, looking him straight in the eye.

He nodded his head once. "Good. That was my only intention. How are you feeling? She said you accepted sedation once you had a ride. I don't blame you. Jay always said those machines were torture."

"Yeah, they … um … had to do my spine and my brain, so it took a really long time. You have to lie so still, you know, so it was probably best. I'm glad Dully could swing by and get your mom after school to take her back to her car. I hope it wasn't too much of an imposition," I told him, leaning back in the chair.

He got down on his knees and crawled over in front of me, taking my hands again. "No, it wasn't an imposition, and you're killing me here. You look so tired and scared. Maybe you should take the day off tomorrow."

"I probably should, but I'm not going to. The hours until Friday afternoon will be interminable enough. Not going to work would just make it worse."

"I guess you're right. Then you better eat this pizza, because you need to stay strong to lift all those bags of flour," he teased, handing me the plate.

I picked up the piece and took a bite, determined to put on a braver face, so he didn't look so worried. "Oh, that is good. I wouldn't have done the green olives, but that's nice."

He laughed his *I'm relaxed* laugh and got a second piece from the box. "It's my favorite version of Gallo's pizza. So, who was it?"

"Who was what?" I asked around the pizza in my mouth.

"Your first date?" He grinned, the dimple that was only visible when he smiled all the way to his ears, winking at me.

"Ugh, Colton Harbor. Do you remember him?"

I laughed as he made the gagging sound with his finger down his throat.

"That guy was so slimy. I couldn't believe you agreed to go out with him," he said, shaking his head. It stopped mid-shake when he realized what he said.

"Oh, really? You knew Colton was my first date?" I asked teasingly.

"No, but I knew you went to the prom with him. I was all *Ewwwww*, when I heard about that." He took another bite of the pizza and glanced anywhere but at me.

"Did Jay tell you about my wonderful lack of judgment? You had already graduated by the time it was my senior prom." I took a bite of pizza and lifted one brow at him as I waited for an answer.

"He sure did. He was seriously disappointed in you," he chuckled.

"To be honest, so was I," I moaned, dropping my head and shaking it. "He thought going to the prom meant an automatic invitation to my bed. I ditched him before the second hour and called my dad for a ride home."

"Good for you!" He did a fist pump and then gave me a high five. "You don't need to put up with a scumbag."

"Versus a Catholic schoolboy?" I asked deadpan, and he held his hands up.

"Okay, you got me there, but I mean no harm, and I brought pizza." He stood up and took my empty plate. "Want another piece?"

I shook my head no and he walked behind my chair and out of my line of sight. I heard him putting the leftover pizza on a plate and smiled when he stashed it in my fridge. When he came back over, he had his coat in his hand.

"There's enough left for you to take for lunch tomorrow. I'll go now, so you don't get too tired. I just wanted to check on you."

I struggled to stand up and he held his hand out. I took it and hauled myself up, the long hours in the MRI machine making every part of my body stiff and sore.

"Do you have somewhere to be?" I asked, surprising myself as well as him.

"Nope, no place, but my apartment."

I pointed at the door. "Would you want to go for a walk by the lake with me? My body is stiff from the MRI machine, and I'm not sure I'll even be able to move tomorrow if I don't stretch it out."

He hesitated for a moment with his hand still holding mine. "I would love to go for a walk, but the lake is awfully far away."

I shrugged and grabbed my cane. "That's true. How about if we drive to the lake, and then take a walk on the path? It's level and there are plenty of places to rest if I get tired."

"You drive a hard bargain, but you've got a deal."

He put his arm around my waist and helped me to the car. This one time, I didn't even mind when he kissed my cheek before he closed the door.

Chapter Eight

I was picking rolls from the bench, six at a time, a little trick my dad taught me when I was barely old enough to stand on a stool, and help him pan them. Pick, pan, proof, the three Ps of baking. My dad always said if you have a good base for every product you sell, then you'll never go hungry, and neither will the town. I guess our bread and bun base was good because I had been doing this as long as I could remember. I just wasn't thrilled that now the pick part took longer since my right hand kept dropping the dough.

I slid the last pan into the proofer and set the timer, checking the oven for the twelve pies I had put in to bake for Kiss's Café. The clock already read five a.m., so I had to get them out and cooled before Millie or April came to get them. After I nearly fell out of the van on Easter, they insisted on picking them up, rather than me delivering their pies. I hated that they felt the need to do that. Maybe after the summer rush, I could go back to delivering, but to be honest, I didn't always have the time. I was too busy. The bakery was so busy that my dreams of becoming a renowned cake decorator were even taking a backseat to buns and pies.

I scooped the extra dough off the bench with my scraper and piled it back up. I stared at the dough, trying to decide what to do with it, and finally grabbed some muffin tins and tossed three round balls into each one. Cloverleaf rolls would be on the menu today at Kiss's Café.

As I rolled the balls, I thought about Bram and our walk out at the lake. He insisted on helping me walk down the smooth, even path with one arm around my waist. By the time we got a few hundred feet, my muscles had started to loosen up and I didn't need to lean on him, or the cane, quite as much. When he noticed me getting tired, he would lead me to a bench where we would sit and rest for a few minutes before moving on.

He showed me his favorite place for wedding pictures, the small bridge that spanned the edge of a creek running off the lake. It was a beautiful spot in the darkness. The moon shone over it just right, so the bridge was awash in light, but the rest of the area was pitch black.

I enjoyed listening to him tell me about his work, and the different photos he had entered in competitions around the country. He was a small-town boy with big dreams. I asked him why he stayed in this little town when his talent was much bigger and his answer was simple. Family. He said, *what good is money and prestige if you're alone in this world?*

I told him he was right. I'm alone in this world

and I have money, but I would much rather have a family, especially right now. That's when he told me his family was my family. He also said that all of Snowberry was my family and I should accept that as fact.

That was easier said than done, though, when you've spent your life being the one who takes care of the town. I've spent my life providing the memories for all of their special occasions, and the comfort food when they were grieving. It wasn't easy to admit that now I'm the one who could use comfort. It's not in my make up to ask for it.

I had better learn to ask, though. If I didn't, I might lose my business. With that in mind, yesterday I called my dad's friend Mark and asked him to come to work for me part-time. He would work enough hours that I could concentrate on wedding cakes and pies this summer, while he did the heavier grunt work of bread and buns.

Mark retired from a bakery in Rochester a few months ago and found himself bored with retirement. He was here a lot talking shop and had even thrown on an apron and helped me pan and pull from the oven.

I think he feels like he's watching out for his friend's daughter. He and my Dad grew up together, and both worked at the same bakery after high school. I suspected he knew I was struggling and that's why I saw him so much now. Whatever the reason, when he comes into work tomorrow morning, I'll be very relieved.

Tomorrow morning.

It might as well be a lifetime away. Looming before me was two o'clock this afternoon and getting the diagnosis I already knew in my heart. What I hadn't made peace with was what happened after the doctors gave me their findings. I was certain of one thing, the clock will keep moving forward and I will still have a business to run and a life to live. Where does something like MS fit into a life like that?

I wish my mom was here so I could ask her. Growing up, she rarely ever talked about it unless she was in a relapse and needed help. Even then, she tried to do everything herself unless she couldn't even stand, then she had to stay home from the bakery and try to recover. I suspect those were the hardest days for her because this place was a second home to her, just like it is to me.

I pulled the fresh pies from the oven and set them out to cool, watching as the steam rose off the pecans that had darkened to a deep coffee brown. The proofer timer went off and I started pulling pans, sliding them into the oven as the wheel spun the racks in a slow spiral. I flipped the oven door closed and set the timer, going to the backroom to get pie containers. Hopefully, April wouldn't come by until at least six, so the buns and pies had ample time to cool before I packaged them. I was no sooner back at the bench when I heard a knock on the back door. Great. So much for that idea. I pulled the door open, already talking.

"The buns are still in the oven and the pies just came out, so ..." my words faltered when I saw that standing in front of me wasn't April, but Bram.

"Buns in the oven, you say? I've heard that usually leads to eighteen years of commitment."

The man was a comedian. "A bakery joke, cute, very cute."

He grinned, doing a little curtsy and that's when I noticed his hands were full.

"What are you doing here, Bram? It's five in the morning."

He stepped forward, and I had to step aside and let him in.

"You Alexander boys are pushy, you know that? Please, by all means, come in." I sighed before I closed the door behind him.

"It's true. If you think I'm pushy, you should meet my dad," he teased.

"Um ... yeah ... I've met him. You know, he's that guy who delivers babies over at the hospital. He also has a real addiction to lemon bear claws."

"All true, but only your lemon bear claws. He says no one else can hold a candle to your pastries. I brought you some coffee," he said, holding the cup out to me. I accepted the take-out cup from his hand and inspected it closely.

"How did you get coffee at this time of the morning? Even Noel isn't open yet." Not that I cared all that much how he got it as I sipped the vanilla nut brew. Coffee was coffee, any time of the day.

He sipped some of his own and set it on the bench. "I know this little place a few miles out of town that's open 24 hours, so I drove out there and got some."

"The truck stop? You drove halfway to Rochester to get coffee?" I asked, shocked.

He nodded a little and shrugged. "I had to take them some printed materials from the paper anyway, so I figured since they were open 24 hours, I could combine the trips and get some coffee for my morning commute."

I took another sip. "They make great coffee. Thank you for thinking of me," I said softly, the silence in the room surprising me for a moment. It was awkward, yet not. Comfortable yet not. It was like there was electricity in the silence I didn't want to touch, but I couldn't stay away from, either.

"You didn't get up at four in the morning just to deliver promotional materials, did you?" I asked, and he shook his head no.

"I didn't actually go to sleep. I was delivering promotional materials at four a.m. because I couldn't stop thinking about this girl who was going through a rough time and had a really hard day ahead of her," he conceded.

I set my cup down on the bench and crossed my arms, leaning my ribs on the bench. "In my heart, I already know the answer, Bram, but I will be glad when this day is over."

"I just wanted to check on you and tell you that

I think you're an incredibly strong woman, considering what you've already gone through in life. I've always thought so, even before all of this. I'm not sure I could go through what you have and still be as positive as you are," he reached out and picked up my hand, holding it lightly.

"Thank you, Bram, but I'm not always positive. Sometimes, I just live on autopilot because it's easier. I do what I have to do and that's how I keep going," I admitted, my voice surprising me when it sounded sad.

He tugged on my hand until his arms were wrapped around me. I instinctively wrapped mine around him, too, and he swayed me back and forth a few times. His hands were warm, even though the morning was cool.

"That makes sense, but I wish it wasn't so. You should enjoy life a little bit. You deserve it," he whispered.

I didn't fight to get out of his arms, which surprised me. "I asked Mark to come and bake for me part-time, so I can have more time to dedicate to my cakes."

He pulled back and gazed at me. "That's great, Liberty. You have a natural gift and creative talent when it comes to cake. I think you're a lot like me in that you know something great is waiting for you if you could just find the time to do it around everything else your job duties require."

I laughed then and it lightened the mood. "You and I might be kindred spirits, Bram. I just decided that if I keep waiting until *tomorrow,* it would never happen. Now, with my right hand the way it is ..." I stopped and he picked it up, rubbing the palm.

"You're afraid if you don't do it now you may never be able to do it?" he asked, and I shrugged a little.

The timer went off to remind me about the buns, and we jumped apart. I pulled the oven door down and yanked the pans out one after the other, stowing them on the sheet pan rack to cool. He was watching me, his blue eyes so intense I wondered if he could see my soul.

When I turned back, he was smiling and didn't try to hide that he was enjoying the view. "I should get back to work. I have to package and stock this stuff then finish glazing the donuts."

He nodded and handed me a card. I read it and it said, *Bram Alexander Photography* and had his cell number listed. He motioned at the card. "I realized you don't have my number, but I want you to have it in case you ever need it. If you need me later, promise you'll text or call?"

I nodded, slipping the card into the pocket on the front of my shirt. I rested my hands on my pants and my fingers encountered the brace, something I still wasn't used to.

"I was thinking about asking you to come with me today, but I know you have to work and I can't ask you to leave. Besides, I know what the doctors are going to say, so I guess it's not going to be a big surprise." I shrugged uncomfortably. Admitting to him that I might need him was almost too much to bear. "Anyway, maybe I'll call you later and tell you what they said?"

He walked over and stood so close to me our bodies touched. "Anything you need, anytime you need it, Liberty. I mean that. No strings attached. Just the caring arms of a friend who doesn't want you to feel alone today, or any day. Okay?"

I nodded my head and forced the tears that filled my throat down and away. His hands came up and cupped my cheeks before he placed a kiss on my forehead.

It didn't feel like something a friend would do, but I didn't mind. I liked feeling safe in this space with him. He hugged me gently, his arms swaying me for just a few moments before he released me and stepped back.

"I'll talk to you later today then, right?" he asked and I nodded.

"Thanks for the coffee and the friendship," I whispered as he walked to the door.

He pulled the door open and stood in the light of the rising sun. "No thanks necessary, Lib, that's what friends do."

Chapter Nine

The doors to Providence Hospital whooshed open and the air blew my hair all over my face. I didn't put it in the usual ponytail I normally keep it in. I remembered how it looked in the picture Bram had taken and decided I wanted to hide behind it today. I left it down to fall over my shoulders to hide my face.

The lobby of the hospital was busy with people coming and going, pushing strollers and wheelchairs. There was one particular wheelchair that made my shoulders sag even more than they already were.

"Hi, Liberty," she said, taking my hand. "Mac, forward, hands," she said and the wheelchair moved forward at a slow enough pace for us to hold hands and walk. I still wasn't used to her research wheelchair that used voice recognition technology to do things for the user. It was something that wasn't even possible just ten years ago.

"Hi, Snow. He told you, didn't he?" I asked, the déjà vu from Wednesday hitting me again.

"He did and he said ..."

"He was breaking his promise to me, but it's

okay because you're a doctor," I finished.

"Mac, stop," she said as we neared the elevator, and the chair stopped.

"No, he said he was breaking his promise to you because someone should be here with you today. Someone who's a friend and cares about you, but also understands what is going to be said in that room. He wanted to come, but since you didn't ask, he thought I should be there instead," she explained patiently.

She let go of my hand and rolled the chair forward to the elevator, so she could punch the up button. I stood behind her and crossed my arms over my chest.

"Those Alexander boys drive me crazy. They're so pushy and conniving," I groaned, hoping for someone to commiserate with.

"They get it from their mother," she laughed, rolling onto the elevator so I could get on, too.

She hit a button and the doors closed in front of us. "I met Dully right here on this very elevator. He wasn't pushy then. He was scared."

"Scared?" I asked, surprised, and she nodded.

"Yeah, the elevator stopped halfway between floors, and he hates elevators. He was pretty nervous standing over there in the corner, holding on with a death grip. That was the start of a beautiful relationship." She smiled and I looked down at the floor until the doors opened.

I almost got off until I noticed it wasn't neurology. "Snow, this isn't the right floor.

Neurology is up two more." I reached my hand out to push the button, but she stopped it.

"We're going to meet in my office. It's more comfortable there." She encouraged me to get out of the elevator and I walked down the hall slowly behind her chair. She pushed the door open and I walked in, the size of the room surprising me. There was a couch, two chairs, and a coffee table arranged on one side, with her large desk on the other, the window behind her chair.

I sat down on the couch nervously since Dr. Hinter wasn't here yet. She moved Mac over next to the couch and transferred onto it, sitting close to me.

"How's Dully?" I asked suddenly, wanting to take some of the attention off myself. "Bram said he's really struggling with something right now. Is everything okay?"

Snow did the so-so hand at me and then clasped them together. "It's a terrible situation that I'm not at liberty to talk about, and one he's not dealing with very well. I think part of it is, he's always had a real soft spot in his heart for this particular student, and part of it is our girls. Everything happened shortly after Jo-Jo was born, and now when he looks at her, he can't stop thinking about what he's dealing with at work. I'm sure you've noticed Dully has a real dedication to his students and to people with disabilities."

I chuckled and nodded. "I have noticed. He's one of a kind, that's for sure. I sometimes wish he was my brother. He always seems to understand when people are having a hard day, and he always finds a way to cheer them. I don't like hearing that he isn't doing well. I hope things get better quickly."

She reached out to tuck a stray piece of hair behind my ear and smiled confidently. "He will be okay. I'll make sure of it. You only need to worry about yourself right now."

"Snow, I know what he's going to say. My mom had MS, you know. This isn't something I've never heard of before."

"I know she did. She was part of the study here at Providence on whether or not there really is an MS gene."

I turned and stared at her in a state of utter shock. "She was? I had no idea."

"She wanted to help others, but that was pretty much your mom in a nutshell, right?" she asked.

"She was something special," I agreed. "She died so long ago I didn't think they were even doing studies on that yet."

"Oh, we've been doing studies on MS for years, hun. We just aren't learning things as quickly as we would like. It's a complicated and diverse disease."

I ran my hand across the back of my neck. "Yeah, Mom had it for twenty-some years before she died. I was always told it wasn't hereditary, but now, I have to wonder."

"The medical community doesn't believe it's

hereditary. The belief is that there is a gene, which has been proven, and if you have that gene, you have a higher chance of it becoming active if something triggers it. If you get the diagnosis, we can talk more about that, but let's wait and hear what Dr. Hinter has to say," she said optimistically.

She no sooner said his name and he walked through the door of her office. He shook my hand and then Snow's, set his computer down on the coffee table, and made himself comfortable in the chair across from us.

"Hello, ladies, it's nice to see you. I don't often get to have consults in this kind of luxury." He laughed a little and Snow did, too.

"I just thought Liberty might be more comfortable here than upstairs," she explained, taking my hand.

"Of course, I don't mind at all. I do have to ask, though, Liberty, do I have your permission to speak with you about your test results with Snow in the room?"

"Um ... yes. Is that a problem?" I asked, looking between them.

They both shook their heads no, but he answered. "No problem at all. I just have to ask because of HIPAA laws, you understand."

I nodded and he opened the computer, typing in what I assumed was my name. I listened as he started to tell me what the MRI showed. How the white spots on my brain and spine were MS plaques, and how that was causing the weakness in my leg and hand. That he felt by adding several medications to my daily routine and continuing with the brace, I would recover from this relapse and go into remission.

"Do you have any questions, Liberty?" he finally asked, and I glanced up into his face, confusion etched on mine.

"Will the weakness in my hand and leg get worse? Will I end up in a wheelchair?" I asked, not even sure where the question came from. I didn't think I had any questions when I walked into the room. I thought I had it all figured out.

"I won't lie to you and say it won't, because it's too early in your course to know that. It's possible that if this is relapsing-remitting multiple sclerosis, which I believe it is, then there may come a time when you need a wheelchair if you are in a relapse, but you have to remember that right now, you aren't being treated. Once we get you on medications to treat the weakness, I'm confident you will see an improvement," he assured me. "Are there any other symptoms that you're having that you think may be linked to what we now know is MS?"

I wasn't going to mention it but then thought better of it. "I'm tired all the time. I always have to take a nap when I get home from work. That's really weird for me because I've been doing bakery work all my life. It's frustrating," I admitted, and Snow squeezed my hand to remind me she was still there.

"That's very common when you're in a relapse of MS. We can help you with that, too. It may take several weeks to several months for you to see a real improvement in the fatigue, though. The best thing you can do is rest when your body tells you to, so you don't wear your system out."

I nodded and folded my hands nervously. "Okay. That's all that I can think of right now. It's just my right hand and my right leg that is really the problem for me at the moment."

Dr. Hinter smiled gently. "I will get prescriptions sent over to the pharmacy like we talked about then, Liberty," he promised, closing his computer. "I want to see you back in two weeks, but I want to hear from you if you have any questions, problems, or concerns with symptoms or medications. You can also speak with Snow if something comes up and I'm not available. She runs our MS research programs here and is very knowledgeable, sometimes I think even more knowledgeable than me."

"Oh, I didn't know that. I thought she just worked on the research program with the wheelchairs," I stuttered, my mind racing.

Snow nodded. "I do, but part of that is hooked in with the MS program, too. Having a chair like Mac available to MS users is part of the program. We can talk about the research programs we have available in a few days once you've digested all the information Dr. Hinter gave you today," she suggested, and I nodded in a daze.

My mind was spinning, but I knew I wanted to be part of helping someone else. "I would like that. If I can help someone else, I want to do it."

She pushed some hair away from my face. "You remind me so much of your mom right now. She said the exact same words to me when I was a brand-new researcher starting out. She would be so proud of you."

I fought the tears that burned behind my lids and didn't make eye contact with her for a moment. I needed to get away from here and take a deep breath to clear my thoughts, but Dr. Hinter's words echoed in my ears. I glanced up at him.

"Are the prescriptions expensive? I mean, I have money, but are they going to be a large bill every month?" I asked worriedly.

He smiled at me then. "For the first time today, I feel like I can give you good news. The medications aren't expensive. Most of them have been around for years, so no, the impact won't be great on your pocketbook, but they will be on your system. There are several new drugs that are being tested as well, but again that's something you can work with Snow on," he assured me.

"I'm sorry, there's just so much to take in. I'm probably asking the wrong questions, but my mind is spinning."

"There are no wrong questions, Liberty. Every question is valid and should be answered to put your mind at ease. Again, contact me anytime or talk to Snow when something comes up. You aren't alone in this diagnosis. I want you to know that. It's not a death sentence, either. We have a good handle on what damage has already been done to your nerves and now we can go forward with treating you. You will have to work around some things, but you can still have a full and active life." He stood then and shook mine then Snow's hand again. He laid his hand on my shoulder. "I wish I didn't have to give these diagnoses, but I will tell you, Liberty, that you've been very accepting, and I know that if we work together, you'll be just fine, okay?"

I nodded and stood up, giving him a short hug. "Thank you, Dr. Hinter. I appreciate your candidness and your reassurance. Your next loaf of apple nut bread is on the house."

He laughed then and shook his finger at me. "You're giving away my secrets, little girl, but I'll be by for that in a couple days. I can promise you that because the one at home is almost gone." He winked at me and waved at Snow, then left us alone in the room.

I sat back down on the couch and looked up at the clock. It had only been an hour since I walked in the door and those sixty minutes had changed my whole life.

"What are you thinking right now?" Snow asked, rubbing my back.

"I was thinking that my whole life just changed and even though I thought I had already put it straight in my mind, I clearly haven't. I'm confused, scared, and a little bit angry," I said honestly.

She hugged my shoulders and nodded. "All normal and understandable, Liberty. You were given a lot of information and not easy information at that. I'm always going to be here for you if you have questions, day or night. Don't be afraid to call me at any time if something comes up, or you aren't sure if it's normal," she told me.

I turned and gazed at her for the first time in an hour. "Snow, you have a family of your own. I can't do that," I started to say, and she held her hand up.

"You can, and you will. I have a family, yes, but I'm pretty good at being a mom, wife, doctor, and friend all at once."

I laughed while holding her hand. "You're saying that you're great at multitasking."

"I have to be, I'm married to one of those Alexander boys," she laughed.

I pictured Bram pushing his way in the door of my bakery this morning, then wrapping me in his arms, and I smiled against my will.

Chapter Ten

Bram

I stuck my hands in my pockets and walked down the path, trying to be respectful of the people who lay under my feet. I could see a figure sitting on the ground a few hundred feet ahead of me and I suspected it was the girl I had spent the last hour looking for.

When I finished work, I went to the bakery and then her house, but she wasn't in either place. I called Snow and she didn't know where she had gone when she left the hospital. Hard as I begged her to, she also couldn't tell me what the doctor said. I was pretty much out of ideas until I stopped long enough to picture Liberty in my mind and where she would go when she felt alone and upset.

That was when I drove to Rest Haven Cemetery and found her Toyota parked near a tree. It was only four o'clock, but I knew the last two hours had been rough on her. I could tell by the way her shoulders were slumped forward and her head hung low over her outstretched legs.

I stopped a few feet away from where she sat, brushing off the grass and old leaves from the headstone of her mother and father.

"Hello, beautiful," I whispered and she glanced up at me, startled. Her face was wet with tears and her cheeks were red. She didn't make eye contact and quickly looked away again, swiping at her face as though she could hide the evidence of her pain.

"Hi, Bram," she said, her voice hoarse. "How did you find me?"

I sat down cross-legged next to her and massaged her back since it was turned toward me anyway. "I tried to think of the most comforting place you would go when you were upset. I played a hunch, as they say in the business."

"I've been here for a half an hour and I want to go home," she whispered.

"Why don't you go home then?" I asked, confused.

"Because I can't get up!" she yelled, but her voice was so hoarse it was barely above normal speaking tones. She dropped her head in her hand and cried sadly. "I got down here and I'm stuck." She hiccupped and her ears turned red with embarrassment.

I circled my arms around her shoulders, resting my chest against her back, supporting her the only way I knew how. "You should have called me and I would have come," I whispered in her ear.

She held her phone up and she had a text message typed out, but not sent. I read it aloud. "I'm at the cemetery and can't get up off the ground. If you aren't too busy, could you come help me? If you can't or don't want to, I understand. I'm sure you talked to Snow and she told you I have MS."

I sighed. "I'm sorry, honey. I haven't talked to Snow, at least not about what happened at the appointment today. I tried, but she couldn't tell me. She did tell me you were upset and I should check in on you after work. For the record, I'm never too busy, nor would I ever not want to help you. Why didn't you send the text? I've been looking for you for the last hour," I whispered, hugging her tighter.

"I'm embarrassed, I guess," she said sadly.

"And confused and scared?" I asked and she nodded her head.

"What did the doctor say he was going to do to help you?"

"He prescribed some medications to help with the weakness and fatigue. I have to pick them up at the pharmacy. I guess I better get over there before they close," she fretted, trying to move out of my arms, but I held her there.

"You have some time, just relax," I soothed.

"Thank you for asking Snow to be there today. God, I hate this," she cried, and I hugged her even tighter, pressing a kiss to her cheek.

"You hate what, Lib?" I asked.

"I hate feeling like I need someone to hold my hand all the time. Like I'm not a big girl and can't do this alone. It's humiliating."

I let go of her and turned her to look at me, lifting her chin with my finger. "You can't look at it that way, sweetheart. You have to look at it as building a support system. A support system that you deserve to have. Let me ask you something. Do you think Snow feels humiliated every time she has to ask Dully to help her do something?" She gazed at me and I knew she was confused, but I pressed on. "Or Jay, when he has to ask December to help him with something? Do you think Snow is humiliated when Dully has to help her take a shower every night because she can't do it alone?"

"I don't know, Bram, does she?" she asked smartly and I shook my head.

"No, she doesn't, and Jay doesn't either. They know the person is helping them out of love and not pity. I know that's exactly how you're feeling, right? Like people are helping you out of pity?" She nodded, her chin trembling and her hands fisted in the grass on each side of her. "Well, they aren't. I can promise you right now the emotion they feel when they help you is love. My family doesn't know how to pity someone. They only know how to love others and help them through rough spots that won't last forever, even if it feels like it will. Does that make sense?"

She wiped her face on her shoulder and blew out a breath. "Yeah, it does. I'm so messed up right now I can't even think straight. I just know that if Snow hadn't been there today, I would be even more confused and messed up. When Dr. Hinter left her office, she stayed for another half hour and talked me through a bunch of questions I had. She promised I could call her day or night, and offered to talk to me in a few weeks about the research programs she is working on. She told me to take some time to grieve for whatever part of my life I felt had changed, and to not feel guilty about that." She glanced at her watch and back up to me. "That means I have approximately twelve hours before I have to get on with my life."

I laughed and ran my thumb down her cheek, wiping away some of the tears from her face. "We have a big day tomorrow."

She nodded. "I have the cake almost done. I just need to add a few finishing touches in the morning, but Mark is coming in to help me do the other baking. I'll be staying and cutting the cake at April's parents' house once the ceremony is over."

I leaned over and kissed her cheek. "That's great because I'll be taking the pictures, and now my favorite subject is going to be at the cake table." I winked and she blushed, even through the redness of her cheeks.

"I'm going to be okay, Bram," she promised me, trying to sound more certain of it than she felt.

I hugged her close to me and kissed her temple. "Oh, believe me, Lib, I already know that. You've never let anything bring you down before, and this time won't be any different. That said, I agree with Snow, take some time to accept how you're feeling, so it doesn't come crashing down on you all at once. Use the support system that is building up around you to help you get through until you feel better. Okay?"

She nodded at my words. "Okay, can we start by getting up? I'm seriously stuck down here."

I laughed with her and lifted her up under her arms, calling on my memory of the times I'd seen Dully lift Snow. When she was on her feet, I held her there, giving her some time to get her leg under her. Once she was ready, I tucked my arm around her waist and helped her across the uneven ground. She didn't have her cane, and something told me it was sitting in her car, where she left it out of defiance to the disease. When we got to her car, she gazed up at me.

"I have to stop at the pharmacy, but then do you want to go get dinner or something?" she asked, and I hesitated a beat too long. She held her hand up. "No problem, it is Friday night and I'm sure you already have plans. I'll see you at the wedding tomorrow," she said, trying to pull the car door open that I was leaning against.

I held her hand until she glanced up again. "I would love to have dinner with you if you don't mind eating hot dogs in the stands. Jay has a basketball game tonight and I promised Sunny I would take pictures of her little Jaybird." I laughed at the nickname and she did, too. I caressed her cheek. "That was the best thing I've heard all day. Your laughter makes me feel a whole lot better."

She broke eye contact for a moment and shook her head. "I just love that little girl and the way she loves Jay. She's the best."

"Don't let her fool ya. She has that Alexander gene in her. She's a real taskmaster when she wants to be. She didn't really give me a choice about the pictures," I teased and she laughed again.

"I imagine, knowing Sunny. If you don't mind me tagging along, I would enjoy coming. I don't want to be home alone tonight and a basketball game sounds like fun," she enthused for the first time since I found her sitting alone crying.

"I don't mind at all. In fact, you just made my night." I grinned and she blushed again. I stepped away from the door and let her pull it open. She sat on her seat but stayed turned toward me.

"I'll meet you there?" she asked, but I shook my head.

"No, I'll pick you up. The game starts at six, so head to the pharmacy and then home to rest for a bit. I'll be there in about an hour. I'm kidding about the hot dogs, too. I'll take you for a decent meal when the game is over at 7:30, but then you'll have to go home, young lady. Tomorrow will come early."

"That's the truth, but I need some distraction tonight, so I'll be ready at 5:30." She turned to put her feet in the car, but her right leg wasn't cooperating. It wouldn't bend and move under the console, so I couldn't figure out how she was going to get it to cooperate enough to drive.

I leaned in close to her. "Okay, pretty lady, I think we need a new plan. How about if I drive you to the pharmacy and then we stop off at your house so you can freshen up before we head to the game?"

She glanced down at her leg and then back to me. "But you have the SUV," she pointed.

"It won't go anywhere before I get back for it later tonight." I pulled her up and out of the seat and walked her around to the other side. She sat and I lifted her leg into the car. I grabbed my camera bag from the SUV and locked the door before I joined her.

I buckled my belt and turned the engine over then took a quick second to check on her. She was crying silently again and my heart broke apart.

I ran my hand down her face, the tears warm on my palm. "It's going to be okay, Lib."

"Thank you for driving me, Bram. I guess I still have a few things to figure out," she whispered.

"But you don't have to figure them out alone," I promised, backing out of the spot and pulling onto the road back to Snowberry.

I reached over and slipped my hand in hers, happy when she squeezed it and didn't let go.

Chapter Eleven

Liberty

The gymnasium at the high school was nearly packed by the time Bram and I got there. "I didn't know that wheelchair basketball was such a big sport in Snowberry."

Bram had my hand and tugged me along the side of the gym. "I know, right? It's really taken off. Now, wheelchair players from all over the area come here to play, and we cheer them on. It's really pretty cool." He grinned and I nodded, his good mood putting me in one.

I caught sight of Sunny and Dully sitting on the bleachers, Dully cuddling Lila Jo in his arms. Snow was in her chair at the end of the bleachers talking to Suzie and her husband, Tom. They saw us coming and Tom stood up and pulled me into a tight hug. I hugged him back, happy to be in the arms of the number one Alexander boy in Snowberry.

I laughed over the din of the gymnasium. "They told you, didn't they?"

He pulled back and took my face in his hands. "They did, but only because they care about you. Anything I can do to help you say the word. Got it?"

he asked

"Got it." I saluted him a little and he winked then sat down next to Suzie, who I smiled at, and she smiled back, probably glad I wasn't mad at her for spilling my not so secret, secret.

Bram put his arm around me and his lips to my ear. "I told you those Alexander men are pushy."

"You got that right, Alexander," I laughed while digging him in the ribs with my elbow until he called uncle a couple times.

Sunny scooted down off the bleachers and ran over to us, jumping up and down. "Uncle Bram, you brought the Belle to the ball!"

Bram looked confused and I took the little girl's hand. "It's a private joke. Since my last name is Belle, she always teases me by calling me the Belle of the ball. Don't you, Sunny?" I asked as she dragged us over to sit at the empty space next to Dully. Bram let me sit on the bottom bleacher and he climbed up to the next one to sit behind me. He kept his hand on my shoulder, though, so I would remember he wasn't far away.

Sunny was chatting excitedly, "What kind of cake are you going to make for April's wedding tomorrow?"

I leaned in close to her. "I haven't shown anyone because it's a big secret, but I might have a picture on my phone," I said slowly and her eyes turned up to gaze at me.

"Can I see?" she asked quietly, looking around for any eavesdroppers.

I pulled my phone out of my pocket and opened my pictures, holding it to my chest. "Can you keep a secret?" I asked and she nodded her head vigorously. "I can, can't I, daddy?"

Dully smiled at his little girl and winked, so I turned the phone for her to see. She inspected it closely for a long time and had the biggest smile on her face. "Miss April is gonna flip when she sees that!"

"I sure hope so. I've worked hard on it just for her and Crow." I smiled as she started flipping through the pictures. I knew exactly what she was looking for, so I didn't say anything. Her little finger stopped and hovered over a picture that had popped up on the screen.

Her mouth opened and closed like a fish and she nearly dropped the phone when she turned to stare at me.

"That's the most gorgeousest cake, ever. Did you make it?" she asked.

"I don't know what cake you're talking about, Sunny," I teased and she aimed the screen at me, so I could see it.

"Oh, that cake. Well, I made one of those, yes, but then I ate it. I was testing it out to see if I could make it right. Do you think I did okay?" I asked and her head nodded up and down like her neck was a bobber.

"You did great! If I was Swiper, I would so swipe that cake," she said softly, her little eyes traveling over the picture, taking in every detail.

"That's good to hear. I was practicing how to make it because I know this girl who is turning five in a few months, and she happens to love Dora. I think I should have it perfected by say, August twenty-first?"

She squealed with delight. "That's my birthday! Are you making this cake for my birthday?"

"You know I am, girl! I always make you whatever your little tummy desires," I laughed and tickled her belly while she giggled.

"It's whatever my little heart desires, silly, and my heart desires this cake!" She clapped and I caught my phone before it hit the ground. "Oops, sorry," she apologized.

"No problem, honey. Why don't you go show it to your mom and see what she thinks? Maybe you should ask your grandma and grandpa, too," I suggested.

She wiggled down and ran away with my phone. Bram was laughing behind me. I turned around and looked at him. "What?"

He held his hands up. "Nothing. I'm just enjoying watching you two girls play bakery."

I stuck my tongue out at him in good-natured fun and then turned back around. Dully bumped my shoulder a little bit while smiling. "Thanks, you made her night, Liberty."

"She's my only co-cake conspirator, if there is such a thing," I assured him, peeking at the baby under the thin blanket she was wrapped up in like a burrito.

"The cake you made for Jo-Jo was pretty astonishing. You reduced my wife to tears when she saw the figures. That takes talent," he shared honestly.

"That wasn't my intention. I just thought it was a great design when I happened across it online. I'm glad you all enjoyed it."

He held the babe out toward me, still cradled in his arms. "Do you want to hold her? I have to run and talk to someone," he said, thrusting her at me. I accepted the pink bundle of warmth into my arms instinctively, since I didn't know what else to do, and he jogged across the floor. In seconds, he was talking to a boy off to the side of the gym as the wheelchair players were coming out of the locker room. Bram climbed down and sat next to me, putting a protective hand on his niece's bottom. She was asleep, oblivious to the commotion around her or the unfamiliar arms holding her.

"She's such a good baby," he smiled, running his finger over her cheek. Her little lips puckered as though she was sucking, and he was already snapping pictures with his iPhone.

"I've never been around babies much. I don't have any cousins or siblings, so my experience is limited to the few times I babysat," I said, less than confidently.

"You're doing a great job from what I can see. Definitely A-1 aunt material in Sunny's book. I'm sure Jo-Jo will feel the same way someday. It isn't always true what they say you know," he paused and I stared at him, confused. "They say you can't pick your family, but sometimes you can," he whispered in my ear and then winked.

My cheeks heated and I brought the baby up to snuggle her on my shoulder. "Who is Dully talking to?" I asked, motioning toward him with my head.

"That's Adam. He's the water boy for Jay's team. He's a Special Olympian, and was in Dully's class until he moved up to the high school."

"Adam McGregory?" I asked and he nodded, surprised I knew the name.

"I did all the rolls and cake for his mom's funeral. Gosh, he must miss her," I sighed, and that happy feeling dissipated a little at the thought of him scared and alone at such a young age.

Bram stared across the floor, lost in thought. "If you want my opinion, I think Adam is what's eating at Dully. I can't say for sure but Dully has always had a soft spot for Adam. He used to go to the hospital and spend time with him when he was sick. I think Mrs. McGregory's death has really thrown him for a loop."

The little girl in my arms squirmed and I broke my concentration on Dully to settle her back down. When I looked up, I saw Adam hug Dully, and then Dully jogged back over.

"Sorry about that. I wanted to talk to Adam for a minute," he said, holding his arms out for the baby.

"It was no problem, Dully. If you don't mind, I would like to keep holding her." With each moment that passed, I felt more confident with her in my arms. I was enjoying holding her and I knew when he took her again, that happy spot in my heart would feel empty again.

"You keep her as long as you would like. The game is about to start, so we will have to stand for the national anthem. Just stay seated with her," he whispered back.

I sighed in resignation. "They told you, didn't they?"

He grinned sheepishly and nodded, then leaned into my ear. "They did, but that's not why I don't want you to stand up with her. She hates the national anthem, makes her scream every time. At least if you're sitting, you can bounce her around until it ends."

I wasn't sure if he was kidding or not, so I went with kidding. Dully still looked sad and I didn't want to look like I was being rude. "Sure, okay, you got it, Dully."

The music started and everyone but me, Snow, and the wheelchair players stood. The singer wasn't even onto *can you see* when the tiny bundle of pink in my arms started to wail. She screamed bloody murder like a thousand bees were stinging her, and I was helpless. I tried to jiggle her up and down, then back and forth, but nothing worked.

I looked to Bram for help, but he was useless with his hysterical laughter as I frantically patted and bounced. Dully was smirking while he sang and then Sunny came running over with a pacifier. I took it gratefully and stuck it in Jo-Jo's mouth during one of her rather wide-open screams. She settled for a couple of beats, sucking a few times and then screaming, sucking, then screaming. I was never more grateful when the song ended.

Dully sat back down and took her from me, settling her into his arm as he swayed a little until she was happy again.

"Good gosh, you weren't kidding," I laughed. "Does she do that with all music?"

"Nope, just the national anthem. It's like how dogs go crazy when they hear a dog whistle. She can't stand it."

"You Alexanders are strange folk," I teased.

"Yes, strange Catholic schoolboys controlled by the devil. You should probably be most leery of that one," he said, pointing to Bram. "He has big ideas. I can tell."

"Dully!" Bram scolded him. "Knock it off, I do not."

I squeezed Bram's knee and grinned at him, and he shook his head, climbing up behind me again to take the pictures Sunny demanded. I watched the athletes on the floor, their chairs knocking into each other as they fought over the ball. I had never experienced basketball quite like this, but it was fun to watch, and the action shots were many and great. I was cheering as loudly as Dully and the rest of the family when Jay made a basket.

I poked Dully in the arm. "Hey, I just realized December isn't here. Where is she?"

"She had to work, unfortunately, but that's the life of a nurse."

While he talked to me, he never took his eyes off Adam by the big cooler. The young man was handing out cups of water to the players as they came off the floor, and he gave them all high fives and pats on the back. Watching him made me see that they didn't need a water boy as much as he needed a team. He needed a distraction from wherever he was in his life.

"How old is Adam now?" I asked Dully out of the blue, and he gazed at me sharply.

"He's almost sixteen," he answered vaguely, and I knew Bram was right. Adam was the reason he was struggling.

"It was a terrible thing what happened to Mrs. McGregory. I can't even imagine how shocking and heartbreaking it was for Adam," I said, shaking my head.

He didn't make eye contact, but he swallowed hard. "I'd been friends with Mrs. McGregory for a lot of years, and you know that all I could think of when they told me she had been stabbed by a patient was, *what if it had been my wife or December?* I can't put that right in my head. I didn't think about her, or Adam, I just thought about my own family," he said, shaking with anger.

I put a hand on his arm and glanced up at Bram, who motioned to Snow behind Dully's back. In a heartbeat, Suzie had the baby, and Tom had Dully by the elbow speaking to him calmly while he led him out the door. Snow turned her chair and followed them out.

I hung my head until Suzie sat down next to me. She put her hand on my shoulder and kept it there until I finally glanced up at her.

"I'm sorry. I never should have said anything," I groaned.

"Don't apologize, Liberty. It's about time somebody said something to him about it. We've danced around it because we weren't exactly sure what the problem was. What did he tell you?" she asked.

I repeated his words, which would be burned in my memory forever. Bram had moved down and sat next to me on the other side, his arm around my shoulders as though it was completely natural for him to have his arm around me.

"That explains a lot," Suzie said her eye on the boy across the gym floor.

The baby started to fuss and Suzie dug through the diaper bag for a bottle. She pulled one out and the baby hungrily pulled at the nipple, her little hands fisted in the air. It wasn't two more minutes and Snow came back through the door. She motioned to Suzie to come over and she excused herself, taking the baby, the bag, and Sunny over to Snow before they all left.

I dropped my head to Bram's shoulder. "I'm so sorry. Now I'm terribly worried."

He kissed the top of my head as the final buzzer rang and Jay's team won the game by four points. Jay ran the chair over to us and skidded to a halt, wiping his face on his t-shirt.

"Dully again?" he asked, and Bram nodded. "How are we going to break through this?"

Bram pointed at me. "She just did, and that's the problem. He told her he feels guilty because all he could think about was his own family when he heard about the incident. You know Dully. He'll work through it and be fine."

Jay turned around and watched Adam high fiving the team as they rolled off the floor. "I sure as hell hope so, because that boy could use a friend right now. I'm going to go clean up and head home. I'll text you once I've talked to him."

Jay wheeled off toward the locker room and Bram stood to help me up. He held my hand all the way through the gym and out into the night. The sun had set and the stars were out as we climbed into my Toyota.

"I'm really tired. Can we skip dinner?" I asked, leaning my head on the back of the seat.

He gazed at me tenderly. "Of course, babe. I'll take you home."

I rested my head on the headrest while I thought about what Dully had said earlier about Bram having big plans. My tired mind wouldn't stop asking the unanswerable question. Just where do I fit into them?

Chapter Twelve

"I love that you close the bakery early on Sunday," Bram said as he parked the SUV in my driveway. "I hate to say I told you so, but I told you there was nothing to worry about."

I shook my head and laughed as we walked to the door. I let myself into the house and he followed, a little unsure of himself.

"I can't believe I just spent an entire Sunday afternoon with the Alexanders." I exhaled a relieved sigh and tossed my keys on the table.

"Believe it. You pulled it off nicely, too. Most people would have gone running when Jay and December started making out at the dinner table, or if not worse, when my dad tossed rolls at my mom because she didn't like his tie."

"Oh, I wasn't leaving. I had to see how that one played out. I've never seen my cloverleaves used as weapons before. It gave me a whole new outlook on bakery goods," I teased him.

He was dressed down in a t-shirt and jeans, which he put on after church. Then he came around and picked me up at the bakery, not giving me a choice about dinner. Lucinda was closing anyway, but I had to attend my first Alexander Sunday dinner in bakery garb.

"If my guess is right, they're still arguing about the tie right now, and next week it will magically disappear when the dry cleaner loses it," he snickered.

"Your mom is a sneaky one," I agreed. "Hey, do you mind if I go change? I smell like a donut."

He came over to where I stood and got in my personal space, leaning his head down near my neck and inhaled deeply. I pushed at him a little.

"What are you doing?" I asked, keeping one hand on his chest.

"I'm smelling you. Donuts are my favorite." He sighed on the words and I giggled awkwardly. "I think you better go change before I embarrass myself and lick you."

I laughed and ducked away from him, his hands reaching for me, but I escaped his grasp. "Okay, I'll be out in a few minutes. I might even shower, so I don't tempt you further," I threw over my shoulder.

He was standing in the middle of my kitchen, looking unsure. "Am I staying?"

I stopped at the entrance to my bedroom. "Do you want to stay?"

"We could watch a movie or something?" he asked slowly.

"Yeah, see what you can find on Vudu. I'll be right out," I promised, then closed the door and leaned against it.

What are you doing, Liberty?

You should be sending him home, not inviting him to stay. It's bad enough you've spent the last how many days with him?

I picked up a clean set of clothes and carried them back to the bathroom. I flipped the lock on the door before I turned on the shower. I stripped off my bakery whites and unhooked the brace around my leg. I was already a pro at making sure I was sitting down before I took it off, so I didn't fall. I transferred onto the new shower chair I kept in my tub and sighed.

When the doctor handed me a prescription for the brace, he also handed me one for the shower chair. He said it wasn't safe for me to be in the shower standing up, especially when I live alone. At twenty-five, that was a hard pill to swallow, but he was right.

I let the water wash over me and work out the knots in my neck. It wasn't easy for me to admit, but sharing Sunday dinner with Bram and his family helped me get my feet on firmer ground. If the week hadn't had been intensely emotional enough, yesterday I had to face April and Crow's wedding. I managed to get the cake loaded and to April's mom's house with plenty of time to spare. It was a beautiful day, and as I set up the cake, one particular photographer enjoyed snapping pictures of every step of its assembly. I couldn't tell him to stop, because he was there on official business, but I felt self-conscious building a cake as his camera whirred.

When I had it together, he came around the back of the table and showed me the pictures in his viewfinder. The finished cake was, without a doubt, my best one yet. It was three tiers, the frosting done in marzipan to look like sheet music, and the notes hanging so it created a border on each tier. The top tier held two marzipan figures; Crow decked out in a tuxedo with his guitar while he serenaded April in her white gown. The final touch was the music notes that floated above them on clear filament. It was the perfect cake for the musician who couldn't sing and the girl who couldn't hear.

Crow and April's love story was very sweet, and there definitely wasn't a dry eye in the house when they finished their vows. They signed their vows to each other while April's dad interpreted them for the guests. As I watched them share the moment in a language only they understood, I realized how beautiful sign language was. Their movements flowed through them and out into the other person, even when they could only use one hand as they slipped the rings on their fingers. When Crow dipped April down to kiss her, I wondered if that was something I would ever experience. Would I ever be a bride and be kissed by a man who vowed his love and his life to me forever? When I glanced at Bram taking photos of the moment, I wanted to believe it could happen.

When the ceremony was over, we spent the

afternoon in the warm sunshine, and I got through most of the day without even thinking about what my new life would be like. The thoughts snuck in a few times, but Bram seemed to notice and he found a way to make me laugh or to share a hug. Once the cake had been served, I really should have packed up and headed back to the bakery, but I didn't. April invited me to stay, so I sat under the tent and watched them share their first dance together, even though she couldn't hear the music. It was obvious she was dancing to the music in her heart and that was all she needed to hear.

When they finished their dance, I found it hard to sit there any longer and watch all the happy people celebrating. It wasn't that I begrudged them for being happy, but my heart and soul wasn't ready to act like I didn't have a care in the world. I was sneaking out when the photographer of the day asked me to dance. I didn't think that was a smart idea, but he didn't give me a choice.

He pulled me into his arms and stayed in the darkness behind the tent, so no one could see us. The song was Elvis, his words about falling in love. I tried to block it out as he tucked me into his chest, as though we did it all the time. It was hard to believe that all these years I've been running from him, afraid of what he would do to my heart, and now I'm running to him. I'm still afraid to get in too deep, but I couldn't convince my heart not to feel what it feels. I've known Bram most of my life, and there's a reason he's still single. That reason might be me. Pushing him away wasn't working anymore and I didn't know what to do about it.

I snapped out of my daydreams and shut the water off. Dully's words from Friday night ran through my mind and I knew he was right. Bram had big plans and I was part of them. The idea made me half-groan and half-laugh in the small room, my heart and stomach both doing a little flip-flop at the idea. I looked at the brace lying on the floor and sighed.

"You okay in there?" I heard him call, and I froze.

"Are you standing outside the door?" I asked, not the least bit surprised.

"Kind of. You were taking a long time and I was worried you might fall," he answered.

"I have a shower chair now, Bram, but thank you for your concern. I was just thinking I didn't want to put the brace back on, but don't have my cane," I explained as I pulled my sweatshirt over my head, and then a pair of fleece shorts over my legs. After a long week, I wanted nothing more than to be comfortable, and the brace was anything but comfortable.

"Tell me when you're dressed," he said through the door.

"I'm dressed, but the door is locked, hang on," I held myself up on the sink and unlocked the door. He pushed it open and stepped in, picking me up off my feet.

"Who needs a cane?" he joked impishly as he carried me to the couch, and set me down gently.

"Not me, I guess," I laughed as he grabbed the remote and sat next to me. He swung my legs up and over his lap then rested his arm on them with the remote aimed at the TV.

"I noticed you like Bond, James Bond," he quipped in a terrible English accent.

"Love him," I answered, slightly captivated by the way he subconsciously stroked my leg.

Bram

The woman I had brought to Sunday dinner was sleepy by the time the movie finished. She had nodded off a few times, and I let her because I enjoyed watching her sleep comfortably in my arms. She had been going nonstop since Saturday morning, and after I dragged her to my parents' place for lunch, she deserved the break.

That said, I had a hard time concentrating on *SkyFall* when she smelled like fresh soap and sweet buttermilk. It was like I was eighteen again instead of twenty-seven. This girl controlled my every thought again. She has always been a siren singing a song to me, but I was no better at ignoring it now than I was back then.

I shut the TV off and the room was dark except

for the light over the oven in her kitchen. It was nearly nine now and I should go home and let her sleep. She was watching me closely under hooded lids and I took her hand. I laid a soft kiss on it that only lasted a moment.

"I really enjoyed myself. Thanks for inviting me to stay," I whispered.

"You enjoyed watching a movie by yourself while I slept, you mean," she teased and I smiled.

"I enjoyed watching you sleep. How about that?" I asked and that made her blush.

"Hey, I meant to ask you about Dully," I said. "I saw you two out on the deck. I wondered if you made him cry again."

She reared up and pushed my shoulder until I fell over to the side, laughing the whole time.

"You Alexander—"

I threw my hands up and kept laughing. "I know, I know, you Alexander boys are so infuriating!"

She started to giggle, too, and pretty soon, we both had to wipe tears from our eyes. She cleared her throat and smoothed out her sweatshirt.

"To answer your question, yes, we talked, but no, he didn't cry," she assured me.

"Well, that's a first," I teased and she stuck her tongue out at me. I went to grab it, but she pulled it back in her mouth before I could.

"He told me he felt like he was having a nervous breakdown because he wasn't able to express his feelings and thoughts to the family. He felt like none of you would understand. I guess when I asked him about it Friday night, the pressure valve just popped off and he let it all out," she explained and shrugged awkwardly.

"He didn't think we would understand? We're his family. Why wouldn't we understand?" I asked, shocked.

She held up her palms. "I don't know. All I can guess by what he told me was that he thought you would look down on him, and think less of him, for being human and worrying about his family, before Mrs. McGregory or Adam. It's almost as though he feels he has to be the big, strong one of the family who can never have a weak moment or you'll all lose faith in him. Like he has to hold the family together."

"That's ridiculous. Completely accurate, but ridiculous," I sighed.

"Yeah?" she questioned and I nodded.

"Oh, yeah, that's Dully. He's always been the protector, even more so than my dad or older brother, Jake. He needs to cut himself some slack. I have to say, if I had a wife who was a doctor, and a sister-in-law who was a nurse, at the same hospital where a woman was stabbed by a patient, my first thought would be about them, too. It's called human nature. It doesn't mean he doesn't care about the woman who died, it just means he loves his family." I ran a hand through my hair, frustrated that he felt he had to confide in an outsider instead of his family.

She's not an outsider, Bram, I scolded myself. *Don't judge someone else's life until you've walked in their shoes.* The old saying my dad always quoted came back to me and I knew I needed to go talk to Dully myself and let him know we supported him one hundred percent. I also wanted to reassure him that there was never a time that he couldn't come to us and let us hold him up.

"I feel terrible," I groaned, and she raised one brow.

"Why?"

"I've been telling you to use the support system that you've built up around you, and I didn't even think to tell my own brother the same thing. He can feel weak and his family should be there to hold him up."

She nodded and held my hand lightly. "I told him that today, about the support system. I asked him why he thought he could be everyone else's support and never need any himself. Apparently, Snow asked him the same thing last night. He told me your dad told him a story about when he was a young doctor starting out with a new family."

My hand faltered as I rubbed her leg. "Really? Did he tell you what it was?"

"Sure did. Apparently, when your dad was starting out as a new obstetrics doc, he had a patient who came into the hospital to deliver. He had taken care of her through the whole pregnancy and didn't expect anything other than a normal birth. That didn't happen, though, and he ended up losing both the mom and the baby during an emergency C-section."

I leaned back against the couch. "Wow. I mean, I know as a doctor there are probably plenty of babies that he has lost, but I didn't know about this."

"I guess he doesn't talk about it much because it was his greatest moment of weakness, at least that's the way he looks at it. Your mom was due to deliver Mandy any day and every time he looked at his pregnant wife, he broke down in tears. It wasn't about the loss of the woman and her baby as much as he was afraid he would lose your mom and Mandy in the same way."

I squeezed my forehead and let out a breath. "Damn, that had to have been a nightmarish scenario even for a doctor. Doctors are still human, but they know all the things that can go wrong."

She pointed her finger at me. "Bingo and I guess from what Dully tells me, that's exactly what a senior doc told your dad. He told him that every man and woman in medicine had felt the exact way that Tom was feeling. You have weak moments because you feel like you failed as a doctor and didn't do your job, but you also know the same thing could happen to someone you love. I guess Tom forced himself to deliver Mandy, just to bring himself back into a normal breathing pattern again. Shaken, but not broken, is what he told Dully."

"Shaken but not broken. That's my dad's favorite line. He's used it multiple times growing up. Especially when Jay came along. I think of that line often when I look at you." I smiled and she smiled back.

She squeezed my hand. "I think Dully seemed more like himself today, don't you agree?"

"He sure did, but you probably noticed the extra seat at the table."

"You mean besides mine?" she teased, knowing I had sprung her attendance on my family.

"Yes, besides yours. I meant Adam."

She smiled brightly at the mention of his name. "He's a sweet young man. I'm glad Jay decided to take matters into his own hands and brought him out for dinner. Sunny obviously thinks he hangs the moon every night, and Adam thinks Dully does, so I think they will help each other through this."

Her face was animated as she talked about my family and I had to rib her a bit. "I noticed Adam hugged on you a lot, too," I harrumphed, crossing my arms.

"Noticed that, did you? I'm the pie lady, and I think he was just angling for more pie." She laughed when I tickled her belly.

"That's possible, but I think it may have had more to do with how huggable you are. I have a hard time not hugging you all the time, too," I admitted, gazing at her like she was definitely a pie I wanted to help myself to.

She reached her hand out to me and I took it, pulling her up and into my chest. "You feel good against me, Liberty, I won't lie, but I know all you need is a friend right now. I can't cross that line."

"How do you know what I need right now? Did you ask me?" she demanded and I stared down into her face. Her eyes were bright and her hair was lying against her shoulders in a way I couldn't resist running my fingers through.

"What do you need right now, Liberty?" I asked.

"Someone to remind me I'm twenty-five and not sixty-five," she whispered.

I didn't even hesitate when I brought my lips down on hers. She fit perfectly against me and I held her head, angling her to rest against my shoulder. She sighed and that was my undoing. I was a goner, forever unable to be with anyone but her. I kept the kiss slow and easy, not demanding or pushy, as she always liked to point out.

If the kiss was to go further than closed-lipped, she would have to be the one to take it there. Her tongue ran along the ridge of my lips, asking for entrance and I did a mental fist pump. Well, hello, pretty lady. I sighed and let my lips fall open then waited for her next move. She hesitantly tasted my lips again until I wound my fingers in her hair. It was as if I granted her permission and she pressed in closer, her tongue roaming unencumbered by any inhibitions.

I returned the kiss, fighting her tongue for the chance to taste her, to brand her as my own. Her hands came up and wound in my hair and

I moaned deep in my chest. I pulled away from her lips and kissed her forehead, keeping her skin against my lips while we both panted for air.

"I guess you told me," I whispered, my lower half well aware of the words she had just said with that kiss. "And you are definitely not sixty-five."

She nodded her head, my lips still on her forehead as she rested her hands on my chest. "I don't like how I feel right now," she whispered.

"Are you sick?" I asked, and she shook her head.

"No, I mean I really like how I feel right now, and that makes me not like how I feel right now," she said, her voice quiet in the empty house.

"Because you're scared?" I asked.

"Aren't you?"

"Yeah, I'm petrified. I don't want to lose your friendship, but I also can't deny that I have feelings for you any longer. I've denied it for too many years, and being this close to you makes it impossible." I kissed her forehead again.

"I assume your feelings aren't strictly platonic?" she joked, and I hugged her to me.

I whispered in her ear. "Did that feel platonic to you?"

She shook her head no and I let her go, so she could sit up. "Thanks for the nice afternoon and evening, Bram. It was nice to be part of a family again for a little while. This last week has shown me I need one more than I thought I did."

I nodded, knowing she was trying to back away from what we were both feeling without being awkward. I brushed her hair out of her face and held her gaze. "You heard what my family said. Anything you need at any time and one of them will be there. They meant that. They weren't just saying it."

She took my hand and held it. "I know. They have already proven that several times over. I'm doing okay, though. As long as I don't think too much about it, I do okay."

I leaned down and kissed her lips, their softness making me want more than I could take. "Come away with me next weekend."

"Excuse me?" she asked, surprised.

"How long has it been since you've had a vacation, Liberty?"

"A vacation? I own a bakery, I don't even know what that is," she answered honestly.

"Exactly. You need a vacation, even if it's just a short one for a weekend. Come with me to an event I have. It's the first weekend of June and the weather is going to be warm. You need to get away."

She hesitated and I leaned back, my hands up in front of me. "I promise this has nothing to do with the kiss or my admittance that I have feelings for you. I'll get you your own room and you can relax and enjoy yourself for a few days in the big city. I have a few things to do here and there, but then there's a nice event Saturday night, and I need a date. Formal and lots of fun, I promise."

"What kind of event in what city?" she asked.

"A photography event in Minneapolis," I volleyed back.

"That sounds fun, but I don't know. I have a bakery to run," she stuttered. "And I have a wedding on Saturday."

"I know you do, but I also know that you have to deliver the cupcakes for the wedding to the venue by Friday, at noon, so nice try," I scolded her.

"Okay, true, but what about the bakery?" she asked again and I leaned forward, the flow of words stopped when my lips crashed down on hers. I owned the kiss this time and didn't give her an ounce of control. When I pulled back, her eyes were glassy and her whole body was relaxed.

"If you want to go with me bad enough, you'll figure it out," I whispered.

Chapter Thirteen

"Seriously, Liberty, go!" Lucinda pointed out the door. "I have the front of the house under control, and Mark has run a bakery longer than you've been alive. Special orders are done and we can muddle through the rest of the weekend without you, I promise." She crossed her heart very seriously.

I scrunched one eye at her. "Hope to die?"

Her ruse to look tough broke apart and she burst into giggles. "I have your number, not that I'm going to call it, but I have it. Go and have fun. Forget about Snowberry while you're off in the big city with a country boy," she shooed.

"Shhhhhhh!" I hissed my finger at my lips.

Lucinda looked around the bakery, which was empty. "Who's going to hear me? Besides, it's not like it's a big secret you and Bram Alexander got something going on," she sang, dancing around the bakery floor.

"Lucinda! We're friends, that's all," I huffed.

She twirled her finger at me and shook her head. "You can almost say that with a straight face. Keep practicing and maybe someday somebody will believe you, but that somebody ain't me, girl." She snapped her fingers like a diva and started gathering supplies to bag the bun order for the café.

"Are you part of the Alexander family? You're almost as infuriating as they are."

"Clearly not infuriating enough for you to leave," she threw back at me, one hand on her hip.

"I'm waiting for my ride," I countered, and she pointed at the window.

"That ride?" she asked and my heart stopped in my chest.

Holy hell, he was picking me up in a convertible. No, that classic black GTO wasn't unobtrusive or anything, Bram.

I swallowed hard when I caught sight of the man who leaned against the car, very Ferris Bueller style. His shades were on his face and the top was down on the car. I was in trouble.

I picked up my bag and stiffened my spine. "Thank you, Lucinda. I shall see you on Monday." I turned on my heel and could hear her laughing as the door closed.

Bram pushed off the car and sauntered over, taking my bag. He also looked me up and down, with his shades still on. "Oh, I like it when you wear a dress. You've got great legs," he whispered with a naughty lilt to it. He pulled me to him and rested his hand on my butt.

I swatted at him until he let me go while he laughed hysterically. "Bram!"

He set my bag in the back of the car and held out his hand. "What? I was giving you a compliment," he insisted, holding the door open so I could sit down.

"You were giving all of Main Street a show," I grumbled. I swung my left leg into the car and he lifted my right leg up and in, then shut the door. I hated that he was always so caring all the time. It made it hard for me to stay mad at him.

He put the car into drive and pulled onto the road. "I see you managed to find a way to escape for the weekend."

"Very funny," I answered, budging him in the arm.

It was funny because he came over to my house every night after work last week to ask me if I had found a way to go with him. The first night he brought subs, the second night Mexican, and by the third night, I agreed to go to Kiss's Café with him. We watched more movies than I've watched in a year, and in general, he's made me feel like I'm going to be okay.

The medication was starting to work. Even though I was still tired and my leg was still weak, my right hand was stronger and lasted longer at work each day. That felt like a small victory when I was working on cakes.

"I can't believe you picked me up in a convertible. Where did you get it?" I asked, and he smiled behind those shades.

"It's my dad's, but he lets me borrow it when

I'm trying to impress the ladies," he said smoothly.

"Oh, so you mean all the time?" I sassed, and he reluctantly held his hand out for me to give him five.

"You get points for that," he admitted. He pulled something out of the dash and handed them to me. They were a pair of sunglasses to match his. "You're going to need these. The ride is long and the sun won't set for another few hours."

He flipped the radio on as we merged onto the highway. He brought the car up to speed in less than twenty seconds and then blew right past the limit, laughing the whole time. What have I gotten myself into?

Liberty

"I can't believe how much fun that was!" I exclaimed when we left the hotel lounge.

He leaned down and kissed the top of my head. "You've never been to a music lounge before?"

I shook my head back and forth. "I've only been out of Snowberry a couple times in my life, Bram. So no, I've never been to a music lounge. It was totally cool, though, and very relaxing. I'm glad you talked me into it," I teased and he laughed.

He had his arm around my waist as we walked to the receptionist's desk. He did have to talk me into it after such a long drive, but I was glad I agreed. Instead of checking in right away, we went straight to the lounge for something to eat. After an extremely long drive, we hit the end of rush hour when we got to St. Paul. I couldn't complain, though. The company was good, the weather was even better, and both of those made up for the bumper-to-bumper traffic. After all the driving, and then a nice dinner and some jazz music in the lounge, it was nearly ten. I was so ready for my room, a hot shower, and a soft bed.

"Welcome to The Grand Hotel Minneapolis, do you have a reservation?" the receptionist asked.

Bram nodded, pulling his wallet out of his pocket. "I sure do. There should be two rooms for Bram Alexander under the block of rooms for the photography event." He slid his card across the counter and she typed into the computer, pausing for a moment.

"I have one room for Bram Alexander. Are you sure they booked two?" she asked, and he nodded.

"I called on Monday and they added a second room for me. Hang on," he dug around in his wallet, pulled out a slip of paper and handed it to her. "That's the confirmation number they gave me."

She typed it into the computer and stared awkwardly at the screen. "Well, that is one of our confirmation numbers, but no room comes up. That's really odd."

"That's okay, just give me a second room now that we're here."

She shook her head. "No can do, Magoo, that's the problem. There are no available rooms. The hotel is booked. I have the first room you booked and you indicated late check-in. My guess is they didn't indicate late check-in on the other one, so they gave it away to someone when you weren't here by six," she explained.

He tapped his fingers on the desk. "That's possible, I just assumed they would attach it to the reservation I already had." He scratched his head and held up his finger to her, then pulled me to the side.

"I swear I made a second reservation for you. Let's get back in the car, and we'll find a hotel with two rooms available," he promised.

I held onto his arm. "Isn't your event here, though?" I asked and he nodded. I felt bad that he would have to drive back and forth because he was trying to keep chivalry alive. "It's not a big deal, Bram. We can share a room, can't we? It's the twenty-first century, after all. I don't mind if you don't."

Relief washed over his face and he kissed me quickly. "No, I don't mind. I just didn't want you to think I was pulling something, because I'm not."

"It never crossed my mind." I smiled to reassure him and led him back to the counter.

"The one room will be fine," I told her and she grinned, making the keys on the machine.

Bram stepped up and pointed at the computer. "Can you check and see if the room you have is handicapped accessible?" he asked.

I stared at him sharply and poked him in the ribs. "Bram…" I tried to say, but the receptionist interrupted.

"Oh, sure," she typed in the computer again. "It has a walk-in shower with handrails in the bathroom and one king bed," she answered.

He grimaced a little, and she noticed. "I have a rollaway bed we can bring in if you would like two beds."

I waved my hand. "No, a king is fine, really, just check us in."

"As the lady requests, I guess." Bram smirked. "Do you have shower chairs? We will need one of those."

I tried to object, but he held up his hand for me to stop. She handed the keys to him and nodded. "Of course, I'll have housekeeping bring one right up."

Bram took the cards and tucked his wallet back in his pocket. "Perfect. Thanks for your help. Sorry about the confusion."

"No, the confusion was on our end and I apologize. Please, let us know if there is anything we can do to make your stay more enjoyable."

We assured her we would and walked to the elevator at the end of the hall. "I'll take you up to the room and then go down for our bags in the car. Are you sure you're okay with this?"

The doors opened and we stepped in, the elevator empty. He pushed the button for our floor and when the doors slid closed, I pushed him into the corner and kissed him, the alcohol in my system making it easy to toss away any inhibitions. I didn't let the kiss linger and pulled away before we reached the floor.

His mouth was hanging open and I reached over and closed it. "I'm completely okay with this."

Chapter Fourteen

I sat in the spa, my feet soaking in a pedicure tub and a warm lavender eye mask covering my face. I was officially spoiled and loving every minute of it. Last night, Bram got our bags up from the car, but we ended up in a heated argument when housekeeping brought the shower chair. I said I didn't need it and he insisted I did. We were at a stalemate until he said I didn't have to use it, as long as I let him hold me up while I showered.

I snickered under the mask when I remembered the smug look on his face when I took the shower chair and slammed the bathroom door. After my shower, it was his turn, and he disappeared into the bathroom while I stretched out on the bed. That was the very last thing I remembered until about five this morning. I woke up and he had both arms around me while he spooned against my back. His breath was warm on my neck and lulled me back to sleep.

The smile stayed on my face when I remembered how good it felt a few hours later when he woke me up with a kiss and told me I should stay in bed, but he had to go off to his event.

I tried to wake up, I really did, but the idea of sleeping in past seven a.m. was far too enticing for a girl who is always up at three. I languished in bed until there was a knock on the door around nine. It took me a moment to get to the door without my brace and when I finally pulled it open, there was a room service cart and a waiter. He had pushed the cart through the door and poured my coffee, then fresh juice from a decanter, before taking his leave.

There was bacon, eggs, toast, and fruit with a note from Bram. It said, *you have a spa appointment at ten-thirty, someone will come to escort you there. Have your nails done and your hair put up, and then come back and rest for a night on the town. I'll see you at four. B*

So here I was in the spa, enjoying every single minute of my vacation. I was unplugged from life and forcing myself to listen to instrumental music through the speakers while I tossed around what kind of style I wanted for my hair. Did I want to go traditional French twist or something more modern? Maybe I should surprise him and do that chopstick thing you always see women wearing on the red carpet. I wonder if women in Japan wear forks in their hair. I giggled hysterically at the thought and clamped my hand over my mouth to keep from disturbing anyone. I had better steer clear of putting eating utensils in my hair if I was going to keep a straight face tonight.

I wasn't even sure what this black-tie event was for other than it was a photography event. As a matter of fact, I don't even know what he's doing today, but then it's not my place to ask. My phone chirped and I moved the mask aside to check it, thinking it might be Lucinda or Mark with a problem. Instead, it was a text from him.

I know you're enjoying your time in the spa. You deserve it! Relax and be pampered. I hope you don't mind I took the liberty (and by take, I mean I would take you anywhere) to send a dress up to the room. The one you brought is gorgeous, but from what I hear, not quite formal enough. I hope you like it because I saw your beautiful face in my mind the moment I laid eyes on it. If you don't like it, ring the concierge and they will take you to the store to return it and pick something else. See you at four."

I sat, holding my phone wondering what the heck was going on. Was the event really so formal that my little black dress wasn't good enough? Then it hit me. My little black dress only came to my knees, and my brace would show the rest of the way down. I bet he got a dress that covered me head to toe, so no one knew. My fingers hesitated over the keys as I tried to plan out a text.

I'm relaxing in a nice pedicure tub as we speak. Does this have anything to do with the fact that my little black dress is short, and my brace is long?"

I hit send before I over-thought the message and watched as a speech bubble popped up immediately, then down, then up, then down, as though he was trying to word his response just so.

I closed my eyes again until I felt it vibrate in my hand and then I held my breath as I read it.

I'm a little bit offended that you asked me that. Considering how I grew up, and what my family dynamics are, you should know that was a low blow that wasn't even close to being on the mark. The fact is I love your little black dress, but I wanted to spoil you and make you feel like the belle of the ball, because that's what we are going to, a ball. If you don't like the dress, you are welcome to return it and find something more to your liking. See you at 4."

I sighed and banged my head against the headrest a couple of times. *Way to go Liberty.* I held my fingers over the keyboard to type back, but thought better of it and hit the phone icon, listening to it ring in my ear.

"Hi," he answered, and I heard the hurt in his voice.

"Hi. I was going to text, but I seem to cause problems when I can't hear your voice. I'm sorry for offending you. That wasn't my intention. I just, I don't know, I'm trying my best to be positive, but sometimes the negative thoughts creep in."

"Negative thoughts?" he asked, and I heard the noise die down in the background as if he stepped out of whatever space he had been in to find a quieter one.

"Yeah, negative thoughts, like *why would a guy like him be with a girl like me?* or *maybe he wants to hide my brace with a long dress because he doesn't like to see it*, but I know that's me talking and not you, so I'm sorry."

"I won't downplay your fears or criticize your worry about the future, Liberty. I would never do that. Do I like the brace? No, I hate it, but not because of how it looks. I hate that you have to wear it and that you have to deal with this, but I know you're strong enough to do it with the kind of dignity many people don't have. You have to understand that I want you with me, Liberty. If I didn't, you wouldn't be here. I don't care if you wear a brace, use crutches, sit in a wheelchair, or do all three because I don't see those things. I hope you understand that."

"I do now, Bram. Again, I'm sorry for being rude, forgive me."

"It's forgotten, babe. Listen, I have to get back to work, but promise me you'll be in the room at four when I get there? I want to spend an hour or so alone with you before we go to the ball."

"I'll be there," I promised and he whispered *see ya* then hung up.

I put the phone back in my pocket and sat up as the pedicurist approached to finish the job. While she dried my feet and began to massage and pumice them, I tried not to think about the fact that I just hurt the man who was trying to make me feel special. I could hear it in his voice and I hated that I was the reason it was there.

Bram

It was almost four and I was glad to be finished with the session part of the day. All of our subjects had been beautiful and were so easy to work with, which wasn't what I was expecting at all. I was expecting uncomfortableness and worry from all of them. I was pleasantly surprised that the day went off without a hitch. Well, except for the uncomfortableness and worry I got from the girl I was trying to please. I zipped the case on my last camera bag and heard *My future's so bright...*

"I gotta wear shades," I laughed, answering the call. I knew who it was.

"You and your shades," Dully laughed. "How's it going over in the big city, little bro?"

"Great, just finished the sessions for the day and now I'm going back to the room for a rest break before we start getting ready for tonight."

"Were the sessions a success? I know you were a little worried."

I loaded my camera equipment onto a cart. "They were very successful. I enjoyed myself immensely, and so did the subjects. I really think Snow should do one," I encouraged and he chuckled a little. "No, I'm serious. I know she obviously isn't going to let me do it, but I have the names of some of the women photographers that were here today. I'll pass them on to you and you can mention it to her. All the subjects had a lot of fun. I think you and Snow should do the couples' session. You would both enjoy it and make some memories for just you and her."

"Okay, I'll talk to her about it, but I think having some of the pictures to back me up might help," he laughed.

"I'll be sure to send some of my best work," I said snootily.

"Okay, well, have fun tonight. Have you told Liberty yet?"

"Nope..." I said slower than I planned and I heard him sigh.

"What's going on?" he asked, and I scratched my temple.

"Can I ask you a personal question, Dully?"

"Of course, I'm just not going to promise to answer it," he said honestly.

"Fair enough. When you first met Snow, was she defensive about being in a wheelchair?"

"I'm not sure I follow, Bram," he said slowly.

"I mean, did she try to act like her wheelchair bothered you, or like you didn't want to be seen with her because she was in one," I explained.

"Oh, that, I see what you mean. To a degree, I guess. I mean, she couldn't hide the wheelchair, obviously, but she did try to downplay why she was in one. She didn't really want to tell me about her polio or let me see her legs. I think she thought if I saw them, I wouldn't stay if that makes sense. I told her that was never going to happen, but then I am a special education teacher and I'm used to just about every situation. You're not. Is this about Liberty?"

I leaned on the cart with both my elbows. "Yeah, she's really taken the MS diagnosis hard, even though she tries to let on she's fine. She thinks I don't want to see her brace, and she tries to act as though she doesn't need any help. Like last night, I asked for a shower chair for the bathroom, and she fought with me about it for twenty minutes."

"You have to understand that Snow had been in a wheelchair all her life by the time I met her. She's a confident woman, so even though she was hesitant about telling me, she knew that ultimately, there was no changing her situation. I'm pretty sure Liberty isn't in that place yet since she was just diagnosed a week ago. She's still bargaining with a higher power that if she does this or that, would they make her better."

"You think so?" I asked, surprised.

"I know so. The thing is Snow is stagnant. She will never get any better, but she will never get any worse, either. That's not the case for Liberty. MS is one of those diseases that runs a different course for nearly every person. That has to be incredibly scary and cause a lot of anxiety when you're only twenty-five. I think she's dealing with it exceptionally well, considering the situation. You have to offer her support the best way you can and the rest is up to her."

"I'm trying, Dully. I really am…" I said, and he hummed 'hmmmm' until I sighed. "I bought her a dress for tonight and texted to tell her. She brought one, but it just wasn't formal enough once I got here and found out more about the event. When I texted her about it, she accused me of wanting to get her a long gown to hide her brace because I didn't want to see it."

"Which in turn made you upset since you were trying to be nice," he deduced and I was silent. "Bram? You still there?"

"Yeah, still here. Sorry, I was just thinking. I wasn't upset as much as offended that she would think I was like that. Especially considering how our family is composed."

"I'll give you a little piece of advice, Bram. Women are really good at pushing our buttons. Sometimes they do it for fun if they're annoyed at us about something, but sometimes they do it because they're scared or hurt. In this case, I think she's both. She probably thinks she can push you away by saying things she knows you won't like because she doesn't want to think about falling in love with you and then watching you leave."

"She's testing me?" I asked like a dunce and heard him laugh.

"Bingo, little bro, she's testing you. She'll keep testing you for a while. Partly because this is so new for her, and partly because she wants to believe you can love her unconditionally, the same way she loves you," he offered, and I shook my head.

"She doesn't love me, Dully. We're just friends," I insisted.

"Okay, go ahead and carry on with that delusion if you want, but I watched her Friday night, and then Sunday at dinner. She definitely loves you, even if she's scared crapless about it. It's certainly no secret you've had a crush on her forever, either," he pointed out and I sighed. "Don't sigh at me. I'm not trying to make it sound like a bad thing. You're soulmates. Deal with it."

"Soulmates?" I asked to make sure I heard him correctly.

"Yes. Your soul has loved her since the day you first set eyes on her, but the soul and the mind are two different things. Once you convince both of them to work in harmony, that's when things get easier, I promise."

"Thanks for calling, Dully. You always know when I need good advice."

"That's what a big brother is for," he assured me.

"Speaking of which, advice that is, how are things for you? You seem better than last week."

"I'm better, Bram. I guess I care a little bit too much about the things no one else even notices. Like no one knew that my first thoughts were about my own family, but I let that eat at me instead of doing the right thing and helping out Adam."

"You've hit the nail on the head there, brother. That said, promise me that you won't ever pull this crap again. We have all had our moments of weakness, and we will all have more as our lives move forward. You probably have a bigger right than any one of us in the family to ask for support when you need it," I paused and heard him sigh in defiance. "Don't sigh at me. I'm not leaving this open for discussion. I'm simply telling you very bluntly that you don't have to be at the bottom of the pyramid holding everyone up all the time. Sometimes you can be the one at the top who gets to be held up by everyone else. Now, that's all I'm going to say about it. "

"Geez, who's the older brother here?" he laughed, but it was awkward and uncomfortable.

"You are, and now that you've come around, I want to say I think Adam is a sweet young man who really could use a mentor like you. You two always had a really special relationship over the years, and I would hate to see that fall apart now. He needs you more now than ever before."

"That's exactly what Snow said." He paused and I chuckled.

"I've always said she's a smart woman, Dul."

He cleared his throat instead of laughing at my joke. "I'm glad to hear you feel that way about Adam. Snow and I … um … we … um…"

"You what?" I asked.

"We were going to tell everyone tomorrow, so do you promise not to say anything to anyone until after family dinner if I tell you now?"

"That's a given, Dully," I promised.

"Snow and I have been granted temporary custody of Adam from the state. We will have six months to decide if we want to keep him as a foster child or adopt him as our own." The words rushed out and he tripped on his own tongue several times.

"Yes!" I shouted, doing a fist pump. "It's about damn time!"

"Really? You mean you're cool with it?" he asked. The tone of his voice was so surprised I could hardly believe he needed reassurance about this.

"Seriously? Am I cool with it? Adam has been part of our lives for years, Dully. Watching him the other night was heartbreaking. He so desperately needed you to comfort him. When he came to dinner Sunday, I was so relieved because he looked happy again for a little while. It's easy to see how much he loves your little family just in the way he pretends to be Swiper to Sunny's Dora and how he dotes on Jo-Jo and Snow. Yes, I'm one hundred percent cool with it, and I'm glad you finally came to terms with it."

He let out a sigh of relief. "Snow said that's how everyone will feel."

"Like I said, she's a smart woman. Trust me when I say that everyone else is going to feel the same way. When does he come to live with you?"

"We get to pick him up in the morning. He

doesn't even know yet. We were afraid if we told him beforehand, he would run away from his current foster home to come here. He thinks he's coming to church with us and dinner again, but we are really bringing him home to stay," he explained and I could almost hear him grinning across the line.

"Good choice on that one. I agree with you, too. That boy would walk ten miles if he knew he was coming to live with you. Maybe you should let Mom and Dad, and Jay and December in on it now. Call up Jake and Mandy, too. Maybe they would like to have a welcome home dinner for him tomorrow, instead of being surprised by the whole thing while he's there."

"Mom and Dad know because of the state investigation. I didn't think about it, but you're right, maybe the others should know, too. I'm going to call a family meeting tonight, but I'll give you a pass. Go and enjoy your accolades, little bro, you deserve them."

I checked my watch and it was a little after four already. "We're going to have a blast, but listen, text me and let me know how it goes, okay? I'm dying to hear their reactions. I know they are going to be as stoked as I am."

He promised he would and I hung up the phone, pushing the cart toward the elevator. My arms were full of gear, so all I could do was press the floor button with my elbow then lean back against the rail for the ride up. Halleluiah. The man finally sorted himself out. None of my siblings were going to be surprised by this turn of events. In fact, they would be thrilled. Good Lord, if we spent one more Sunday dinner like the last few, someone was probably going to peg him with one of Liberty's cloverleaf rolls.

I laughed into the empty space because my heart was relieved and happy at the same time. The ride to the room was short and as I slid my key in, nerves took over a little part of me. Why I didn't know, except that all I could think about was what Dully said about soulmates.

I pushed the cart through and then off to the side of the room. I stopped by the edge of the bed, but she had her back to me. Her body was wrapped in one of the hotel's terry robes and her hair was pulled up in some kind of twist that knocked the air from my system. She turned over and smiled. It was a soft, loving smile that made me scoop her up and swing her around.

"I'm so happy right now," I whispered into her neck and hugged her tightly to me as her feet dangled off the ground.

She held onto my neck and tucked her chin over my shoulder. "How come? Did you have a good day?"

I set her back down on the bed. "I had a great day, and then I talked to Dully and he made my day even better. The cherry on the cake was when I came up here and saw you. You're so beautiful I can hardly stand it."

She was smiling wide and it matched the one on my face. "What did Dully tell you? Is he feeling better?"

"He's feeling great, and he told me I'm going to have another nephew. Finally, he got himself figured out."

She put her hands on my chest. "Whoa, slow down there, Uncle Bram. There is no way Snow is that far pregnant again. Lila Jo is only a month old. December?"

I laughed happily and sat next to her, so I could hug her again. "No, well, I don't think so anyway, they haven't said they're pregnant. I'm talking about Dully and Snow. Tomorrow morning, they're going to pick up Adam and he's going to live with them. In six months, they can decide if they want to adopt him or keep him as a foster child."

"Yes!" She gave a fist pump, and I laughed even harder.

"That was exactly my reaction, babe. I tell you, that man is smart, but he sure is slow sometimes. I'm so relieved that Adam will have a chance to be happy again, and Dully and Snow have more than enough love to share with someone who needs it so much. My heart is just kind of floating around in my chest."

She cocked her head. "I can tell. I'm really happy for your family. I didn't have you pegged as the most easily moved kind of guy, but maybe I was wrong."

I took her hand and kissed it. "When it comes to my family and the people I love, I am. Maybe part of it was how I spent the day today, but I just never felt as good as I did when he told me about Adam."

She laid her hand on my thigh and I put my hand over hers, so the heat from her hand soaked into my leg. "What were you doing today? I've been curious."

I turned toward her and rested my leg up on the bed a little more. "I was doing multiple boudoir sessions."

Her smile faltered a little on her face and she cleared her throat. "I see. That was exciting, I bet."

She tried to get up, but I held her there next to me. "No, you don't see, but you will tonight. I was working with a renowned group of photographers who put together an event today for disabled women. We did boudoir sessions in several of the handicapped suites. We did some glamour sessions, several couple sessions, and we even did one maternity session. I was a little nervous about how it would go, but everyone had a good time, and we got some great photos for these beautiful ladies to have as a keepsake."

She stared at me intently. "I didn't know you did those types of photos."

"I don't usually, but I have to tell you I think I'll be doing more in the future."

Her hands were folded together tightly, leaving white knuckles on each hand. "Kind of hard to resist spending the day in the presence of naked women, I suppose."

I crossed my arms over my chest. "Not at all the reason why, Liberty, and for the record, they were covered, and the pictures are in no way obscene. When I met these women as they first came in, some using wheelchairs, other's crutches or canes, it was easy to sense that they didn't feel like they could *pull this off*, which was a phrase I heard over and over again today. Anyway, it was a great feeling to watch them as they began to gain confidence that they could. They were sexy and their partner didn't see anything but the beauty they exuded in those photos. Maybe you'll understand it tonight. There will be a slideshow at the event," I explained.

She stared down at the floor and nodded. "I get it, sorry for assuming anything other than what it was. Not that I really have a right to assume anything. I don't own you, nor do I own how you get to feel about any other woman. I was just surprised because I didn't know they did those photos for the disabled. I figured you were spending the day with gorgeous models with bodies to die for."

I held my finger to her lips to quiet her. "Dully thinks we're soulmates."

She glanced up sharply and I smiled while my hand caressed her cheek. Her eyes were wide and showed me that she was scared not of my words, but of the idea that they were true. I leaned in and kissed her, my lips reveling in the feeling after spending the day apart from her. I couldn't stop my tongue from pushing the limits of her acceptance. After a few low moans from her, she opened her mouth and let me in.

I slid off the bed and knelt, now below her, so she didn't have a choice but to be the one to take control. She took my face and held me, so she could deepen the kiss. She did things to me way down deep in my soul, and I knew he was right. I climbed back on the bed and pushed her backward, my hand behind her neck. Her robe had fallen open enough that I could see the white flesh underneath, and I slipped my hand into the crease of the robe and caressed her chest. She moaned loudly and my lower half reacted immediately. So much so I had to roll to the bed, so I didn't scare her.

I finally pulled away from her lips and kissed her neck and then down to her chest, where my hand rested on her heart.

We were both breathing heavily and her face looked dreamy and relaxed. I pulled her upward and onto my lap.

"Dully told me he sees it when he watches us together. I want to explore that idea a little later, but right now, I have to go take a very cold shower and get ready for the evening."

She nodded her head while she straightened her robe and then cleared her throat. "I'll put my dress on while you're in the shower." She smiled shyly, and I leaned in and kissed her lips once. Just enough to feel the softness again.

"Did you like it?" I asked, and she laughed softly.

"No, I loved it. It's beautiful, and I had no idea I would look that good in emerald green. I can't wait for you to see me in it." She winked, and I rubbed the front of my pants a little, groaning. I already knew how I would react.

"Am I going to need another cold shower after I get done with this one?" I half-joked and she stood, smoothed her bathrobe, and then walked away. She paused to look over her shoulder for a moment.

"Oh, yeah," she said, her grin sexy and filled with steam.

Chapter Fifteen

Liberty

I sat next to Bram at the table, our hands twined together where no one would see us. He was so handsome in his tuxedo that I was the one who needed a cold shower when he came out of the bathroom. I wasn't so naïve that I didn't see him react to my dress the same way. Not only had he bought the most gorgeous beaded gown, but he had them send a matching pair of ballet flats. They were exactly my size and my brace fit in them perfectly. He managed to make me feel beautiful and sexy without the danger of falling.

I leaned my head against his shoulder and his arm came up around mine as he listened to the speaker. We had finished dinner, and now they were discussing the events of the convention that had gone on over the last few days.

I focused on the speaker as he started to talk about the boudoir sessions. "Today, we had a well-renowned group of photographers from our association hold a first-of-its-kind event. I don't want to call it a social experiment, yet in a way it was. Boudoir photography has become more and more popular, but today these photographers took it to a whole new level."

The lights went down and I glanced up into Bram's face, a smile tipped his lips as a screen lit up behind the speaker.

"I could explain it, but we're photographers and we speak through images. Enjoy the slideshow." The speaker ducked out of the way of the screen just as music started to play.

The song *You Are So Beautiful* filled the room, and the lights went out completely as the first slides showed the photographers setting up in the rooms, drinking coffee, laughing with each other, and doing light checks. I saw Bram in a new way. I watched the screen and saw through pictures what I've seen multiple times in real life. I saw the way he sees life through his lens, but also the way others see him as a photographer. When the first woman flashed up on the screen, there was a collective *wow* that rippled through the room.

The slides highlighted each photographer, watching them work as pictures of the photographer themselves were taken from behind. It was a fascinating look at photography in a way we never see as the public. Then Bram flashed up on the screen in black and white. He was speaking with a woman in the session, and I focused on the looks passing between the woman and him. It was as though she was a canvas he was about to paint, but not before he knew exactly what she was feeling.

That slide disappeared and was replaced with him kneeling on the floor as he looked through the viewfinder of his camera, and again the photo was taken from behind him. You saw the side of his face and the image in the camera. It was the woman in the arms of her partner as he carried her to the bed. Each new slide went across the screen, but all I could see was the one of him looking at the viewfinder. From the side, you could see how proud he was that he had captured trust in the way she held her partner's neck. How he had captured the look of lust in the eyes of the partner that carried her. Mostly, it was a look of wonderment at how he had captured love as a tangible object.

He leaned over and whispered, "Tenderness, love, trust, peace, and acceptance."

I nodded and laughed because, as usual, he was able to read my mind. He always knew what was going through it at any moment in time, and it made me think of what he had said in our room earlier. We were soulmates. Before I had time to carry the thought further, the lights came up. When the round of applause had died down the speaker stepped back to the podium.

"Absolutely stunning work. I applaud each and every one of these photographers for their dedication to capturing the human spirit in their lens, time and time again. In fact, that leads us to our final award of the night, before we get to loosen our ties and have a little fun." The room laughed as the speaker was handed a crystal camera, some type of wording etched in the glass.

He set it on the podium in front of him so we could all see it. "Every year, the association holds a photography contest. We accept submissions, pick semi-finalists, and then display the images for several weekends where the best of the best vote for their favorites. The votes are then tallied and the winner is awarded the Steven L. Ray Award for Extraordinary Photography. We had so many quality pieces submitted this year that it was difficult to choose the semi-finalists. However, one photo stood out amongst the many to me, and I'm pleased that, in fact, it is this year's winner. Tonight's recipient is a newcomer to our association, but not to photography. He grew up in a small town, and was known to always have a camera to his eye from the time he was old enough to carry his mother's Polaroid."

The room laughed and I turned to Bram. His eyes were focused on the speaker and he wouldn't make eye contact with me.

"As you know, photography is an art, something you must have an eye for before you can be trained in the technical aspects of it. Tonight's winner makes photography an art form, as you saw in that slide show just moments ago. Bram Alexander resides in Snowberry, Minnesota and his passion is wedding photography, but after watching him today, I think he may have found a new art form to add to his portfolio."

The screen behind the speaker lit up with a

photo of Noel and Savannah. I held my breath at the beauty of my friends standing on the bridge he had shown me in Snowberry Park. His hand squeezed mine and I tore my eyes from the photo to connect with his. He smiled sheepishly and I leaned in and kissed his lips. I didn't even care if anyone saw us. The room had the same reaction as I did to the photo, though many had already seen it, I was sure.

"Bram's eye for the beauty of his subjects is second to none. In the essay he submitted with this photo, he tells us this, *"When I took this photo, I was working quickly to get Noel and Savannah centered on the bridge for when the moon would come out from behind a cloud, and bring natural light to the shot. What happened next was something I couldn't predict. This is the type of photo that is created by no one other than the master above. Savannah is turned into her husband, and you would never guess the other side of her face is pulled back in a painful grimace from a nerve condition caused by the fist of another human being.*

Instead, what you see in the very moment this shot was taken is trust in the man standing with her to never hurt her, and always love her, as they had just vowed moments earlier. The moonbeam you see falling across their shoulders is a blessing to this union.

I'm forever grateful to be the one who documented this moment for my friends. I don't expect to win this award, but when I saw the photo in my viewfinder, something stirred inside me. The start to a brighter future for Noel and Savannah, and hope for love and life, everlasting. I respectfully submit Moonbeam of Hope for consideration of the Steven L. Ray Award."

I watched Bram's face as the speaker read his words and saw a side to him he doesn't often let anyone see. I also saw that he was nervous, so I squeezed his hand under the table and he squeezed mine back.

The speaker held up the award. "This photo, technically speaking, is top of the line in concept and execution. From the human perspective, it is one in a million, without a doubt. The words written about the photo indicate professionalism, and dedication, to the art that he so finely practices, as well as an understanding that sometimes, as photographers, we are simply the one chosen to capture a moment that is bigger than us. So, Bram Alexander, you may not have expected to win this award tonight, but you have and, in my personal opinion, it will be one of many to come in the future. Please come up and accept your award."

Bram leaned over and kissed me gently, then stood and straightened his lapels. The rest of the room stood as well and clapped as he climbed the stairs to the podium. He accepted the award and shook the president of the association's hand before stepping up to the microphone.

"Thank you all so much for this opportunity and for this award. I'm not sure I can call myself an artist so much as an illustrator of the beauty that naturally surrounds us. I've learned so much from all of you, and I know I just got incredibly lucky with this photo. I'm thrilled so many people will get to see the love these two people share, and by the way, they are expecting their first baby in November," he told the crowd and a new round of applause filled the room.

When it died down, Bram's smile went from one ear to the other. "I grew up in the kind of family that nurtured our natural talents in such a way we didn't even know it was happening. That Polaroid camera was what I used to document my own life. It was what I used to take the first picture of my baby brother in the first wheelchair he could push himself. He was four and I was five, but I knew even at that young age it was an important moment in our lives and deserved to be captured. The year I turned six was when I got a 35mm camera that I used to take pictures of my brother, Dully, pushing my brother, Jay, out on the ice in a lawn chair, teaching him how to play hockey. I'm pretty sure my parents spent a fortune in film developing, but with each roll, I got a little better and understood a little bit more about the skill that goes into capturing the memories of our lives. I'm grateful for my family because they were my best subjects as I grew. In fact, they still are to this very day. To the professionals who have helped me hone my skills, including all of you who showed me so many new skills today, I want to say thank you. I've learned invaluable lessons that I will take back to my little hometown and use to teach someone else. I'm also grateful to a special lady who agreed to come all the way to the big city with this small-town boy tonight without knowing the real reason why, but also for not asking. Your support of my family and our town over the years is the reason why we can support you now," he finished, blowing me a kiss as the room stood and clapped.

He shook everyone's hands on the way back to the table, but he only had eyes for me.

Chapter Sixteen

Bram

I helped Liberty to the bed after she finished in the shower. She was exhausted and barely upright, her right leg Jell-O underneath her.

"I think we stayed too long at the dance," I joked, as she gripped my lounge shirt.

"I was having too much fun to leave. The music was fantastic and the company, even better." She smiled up at me and I leaned down and kissed her nose. I knew if I kissed her lips, she would fall down before the kiss ended.

"Let's get you in bed, babe," I encouraged as I helped her sit down on the edge. It was so high she couldn't get up on it without a stool or a push, so I helped her until she was able to scoot up and stretch out. "Are you in pain?" I asked, unsure why I was worried.

She took my hand in hers. "No, of course not. It doesn't hurt. I just have weakness I can't control. The medication is helping, though. I can go longer before I get to the point I need to rest. Have you noticed?"

I climbed over her and lay next to her on

the bed. "I've noticed your hand is stronger when you've squeezed mine the last few days. I like that."

She smiled brightly, one of the first few real smiles I'd gotten from her in a while. "I feel like that's a good thing."

I leaned up against the headboard and pulled her up to me. She rested her head on my chest naturally. "No, it's a great thing. Just like having you with me this weekend is a great thing. Having dinner with you and watching you eat without your hand shaking from fatigue is a great thing. The greatest thing was having you with me when I accepted the first award of my career. Those were all really great things, but lying here with you is even better."

She gazed up at me and reached out to run a finger down my cheek. "I'm so glad I found a way to come." She winked and I turned my head to kiss the palm of her hand.

"Me too, babe. It's always more fun to experience something like that with someone important in your life. Makes the memories so much sweeter."

"I get why you didn't tell me what it was about now. It was a lot of fun to be surprised by the events of the weekend. Do Savannah and Noel know you won?" she asked.

I chuckled. "No. No one knows but you, me, and my family in Snowberry. I gave Noel and Savannah a poster-size version of that shot and told them I had entered it in the competition. I'm sure they will be excited to hear, but it's too late to call them now. When we get back to Snowberry, do you want to go with me to bring them the award?"

She sat up and stared straight at me. "You're giving them the award?"

I glanced at the glass camera sitting on the table and shrugged a little. "Seems like that's where it belongs? It's their love story that made it happen, after all."

"That's very selfless of you, Bram. I think if I won an award like that, I would want to keep it," she admitted and I shrugged again.

"I will offer it to them because they're my friends and they mean a lot to me. The thing is, I really just lucked into that shot. They're the reason I won it and I give credit where credit is due."

"You're too humble, Bram. When I look at the photo, I picture it being the moment they both admitted in their hearts they had fallen in love with each other," she sighed dreamily.

It was my turn to sit straight up. "What?" I asked, dumbstruck.

She grimaced a little at the tone of my voice and then her eyes dilated at the look on my face. "Oh, no, you didn't know."

"Know what?" I asked, and she tapped out a rhythm on her thighs while she put her thoughts together.

"That their marriage was meant to be one of convenience in the beginning. Noel was going to marry Savannah so she had medical insurance and could get treatment for her face. She was in so much pain she agreed because she couldn't figure out any other way to pay for the surgery. That's why they got married so quickly."

I leaned back against the headboard. "Whoa, totally knock me over with a feather. Have you seen the two of them together?" I asked and she nodded. "I guess they were the only two who didn't know they loved each other. The rest of us could see it as plain as the nose on our face. How do you know all this?"

She grinned. "I'm the baker. I know everything."

"Not everything," I said softly.

She cocked her head to the side. "What do you mean?"

"I mean that you don't know I've had a crush on you since third grade, at least, if not longer." I gave her half a smile. "There, now you know everything."

She laughed loudly and it made my belly flip with anticipation. "Bram Alexander, I already knew that, too. Well, okay, maybe not about the third-grade part, but you've been trying to take me out since I was old enough to date."

I nodded, picked up her hand, and kissed the back of it. "And why do you think that is?"

She shook her other finger at me. "That's the part I can't figure out. Maybe because I make sweet confections you can't resist?"

I leaned in and kissed her gently. My lips lingered long enough for her to believe the next words out of my mouth. "Not exactly, though, I do love your sweet confections. The truth is, what I can't resist is you. Everything about you makes me a little like a donut-starved teenager."

"You're saying I'm irresistible in a long john sort of way?" she asked, and I laughed at her silliness.

"That's what I love about you, you can work bakery terms into any conversation," I teased.

She froze. "And by love you mean *find amusing*, right?" she asked. She even used air quotes to make her point.

I glanced down at the bed for a second and then back to her bewitchingly beautiful blue eyes. "No, I mean that's what I love about you. I love you, Liberty Belle. You, not your bakery. I could live without seeing your bakery, but I couldn't live without seeing you."

She ran her hand down over her throat nervously. "Wow, Bram, I…"

I held up my hand. "It's okay. You don't have to feel awkward about this. I know I just threw it out there and you weren't really prepared. I didn't fully come to the realization until today when Dully said that to me on the phone. Then your words made me think of it again just now. See, Dully said that everyone can see how much I love you but me. Tonight, when I was standing up at the podium with my eyes locked on you, I knew it was true. I do love you. It isn't just some elementary school crush that's going to go away because I'm all grown up now."

When I paused to take a break, her lips came down on mine and her hands wound their way into my hair. She broke the kiss but kept my face close to hers.

"I love you, too," she whispered, as my eyes immediately locked in with hers.

"You do?" I asked, stunned, and she laughed from the bottom of her soul.

"You sound surprised, but the truth is I knew it when you were standing in my bakery and your laugh made my belly do this weird flippy thing I hated and loved, at the same time."

She sighed and I lowered my lips to hers again. She whimpered under my lips and when I pulled back, her face crumbled.

I pulled her into me and held her. "Oh, Liberty, please don't cry about it. I know I can be a real pain, but I'm not that hard to love," I teased. She laughed, but tears were still falling. "What's the matter, babe?" I asked. I gave her some time to think while I held her for comfort.

"What's the matter? Everything. The way you call me *babe*. The way you take care of me and put me at ease. The way you think you want to be with me, but you just don't understand the implications of that," she answered sadly.

I leaned her back against the pillows on the headboard. "Okay, slow down. You don't like being called babe?" I tried to joke and she half-laughed, half-sobbed. I held both her hands in mine and brought them to my lips. "What implications don't I understand?"

"The implications that makeup MS, Bram," she answered. "It's not like Jay or Snow where you know what you're getting when you get involved. This is a different kind of disease, and it's too early to know how it will affect my life. It's too early to know if my leg will keep getting worse, if I'll be able to keep working, or if I'll be able to have kids. I find it all very confusing and hard to process, and I'm the one with the disease. I can't ask you to go through it, too."

"Do you think that's what your mom said to your dad when she found out she had MS?" I asked.

"That's different, they were already married," she said sadly.

"They hadn't been married for long when she was diagnosed. She had MS all but maybe a couple years of their married life. They got along pretty good if you ask me. Look at what they did together." I gave her a cheeky grin while I massaged her foot. "It's funny that you should bring this up because I asked Dully today if Snow felt the same way when he met her. He said she did, to a point. Apparently, she didn't want to tell him about her polio, how she got it, or what her future would look like, so he made her open up to him. In our case, I'm fortunate to be here to live these early days with you. I want to be the one to help you through them. If we can be in love right now, in this very instant, when there is so much uncertainty, then we can stay in love through anything. If we can come together when it's hardest for you to admit you need someone, and I can love you without a second thought knowing what I know, then we can do that no matter what our relationship goes through." I crawled up closer to her and wiped away the last few tears from her face. "There are so many facets to who you are, Liberty. Yes, the MS is one of them, but it's not the most important one, not by a long shot. I fell in love with you when you were a little girl in glasses who called me a doody head. The MS isn't going to stop me from loving you now when you at least call me by my name."

She shook her head at me, trying to keep a smile from tilting her lips. "You Alexanders' were always so…"

"Pushy!" I grinned, pushing her all the way to her back so I could kiss her lips, all the while tasting her salty tears. I kissed my way down to her neck, my heart in love with how she tossed her head back and let me get into the deepest hollow, then moaned a little as I nipped at her earlobe.

My lips trailed their way down to her chest, parting the robe she wore after her shower, never more pleased to find nothing else under it. My lips skimmed down the top of her left breast to the center of both, where her heart thudded under my lips. Her hand twined its way into my hair and tugged me back to her mouth. She hungrily accepted my lips and returned the kiss eagerly, and full of heat.

I tugged the clips from her hair, so it fell around her shoulders and shone in the light from the lamp. "You're so beautiful, I can't take much more without touching you, tasting you, and being part of you in every way."

She reached for me and I leaned over her, letting my lips linger along the edge of her breast, listening for her cues that would tell me she accepted my want for her. She squirmed under me and I moved my lips closer to her nipple until I closed them over it.

Her fragility was so evident it made me want to treat her like a China doll. All gentleness, all the time. I sucked lightly, while my hand found her other breast and I cupped it. I waited for her reaction and was thrilled when her low moan filled the room. The sound ramped me up to a fevered pitch I could barely control. I wanted to lose myself in her, but I didn't, afraid I would scare her.

I pulled her nipple through my teeth gently, nipping lightly until her breath caught in her chest. I moved to the other side, lavishing that nipple with the same kind of attention. She had her hands in my hair and was calling my name softly, pulling me toward her. I went to her, swallowing her words with my lips, and answering her pleas with my tongue.

She ripped her lips from mine, her breath heavy and her eyes hooded. "We have to stop,

Bram. I'm not prepared."

My hand hesitated on her breast, where it massaged her gently. "I am," I admitted. "I picked some up today, not because I assumed we would, but because I didn't know if I could stop myself if you gave me the opportunity. Holding you in bed last night almost drove me mad. I didn't want to get caught with my hand in the cookie jar and not be able to eat the cookie." She bit her bottom lip and looked unsure. "You're in control here, Liberty. This is your call, but if the only thing holding you back is birth control, I've got it covered."

She nodded and reached for me, but I resisted and sat back on my knees. "It's not just about the birth control, is it?"

She shook her head while her eyes focused over my shoulder at the TV on the desk. I took her hand and forced myself into a timeout my body didn't want to take.

"I've never actually gone all the way before," she whispered and my fingers faltered against her palm. "I want to, but I know you're more experienced than I am. I want to make you feel good, but I don't know how."

I pushed her hair back over her shoulders and forced myself to take a breath. I wanted to see her eyes and watch the honesty on her face. I didn't want her to think she could ever hide from me.

"I have some experience, and for that reason, I can tell you this isn't a test. It isn't about mastering a skill, like riding a bike or making cookies. Making love doesn't need experience or knowledge. When it comes to making the person you love feel good, it comes naturally if you understand them in your heart. You don't need experience to make me feel good. You know my heart," I tried to explain, but it was clear I was just confusing her more.

"The other women you were with, did you understand their heart?" she asked.

I shook my head no. "I thought I did, but I didn't."

"So, you didn't make them feel good?" she asked and I laughed, stretching my legs out and pulling hers over mine.

"Not the first couple of times, no. The first couple of times, I was learning how to make them feel good."

She waved her hand. "You just said that you didn't have to learn how to make someone feel good."

"I said you don't have to learn how if you understand their heart. If you don't understand their heart then, first of all, you aren't making love, you're having sex. Second of all, you have to learn how to make them feel good because your heart doesn't already know."

She trailed her finger over my stomach absently. "So why didn't you understand the other girls' hearts?"

"Because they weren't yours," I answered honestly. "It took two different girls to figure that out, but after I did, then I steered clear of dating for a long time. It's not fair to ask another girl to fight a ghost they can't see." I sucked in a breath when her hand worked its way under my shirt and rested on my belly.

"I'm not a ghost. I'm right here. I've always been here. You didn't talk to me or come into the bakery for months," she said sadly.

I lay down next to her, caressing her cheek. "That's because I was trying to rid myself of your ghost. I was trying to convince myself I could fall out of love with you before I even admitted that I was in love with you. I failed miserably at it. I kept fighting this desire for a Bavarian cream bear claw that couldn't be satisfied from anywhere but the Liberty Belle."

She tried to pull her hand away from mine, but I held it tightly. "I thought I scared you away," she sighed, possibly out of sadness, or possibly out of relief.

"How would you scare me away?" I asked, the desire to understand her overpowering my need to hold her.

"When my dad died, I lost every last vestige of love I ever had in the whole world, except for you. Every time you came into the bakery, you would hug me, and it would get me through until the next time you came in. I was so grief-stricken I couldn't talk about it, but those hugs were the only thing holding me together. Then one day, you were gone. I thought I was too needy for you, or too damaged. Of course, at that time, I had no idea what being damaged really was because three years later, I'm far more damaged than I was then, but you're lying next to me anyway."

I ran my hand down her cheek, and she kissed my finger. "You aren't damaged, babe. You just have another facet to add to the beautiful diamond that you are. If I had known what you just told me, I never would have stayed away. I would have come in every single day to hug you and tell you I loved you, even if you couldn't return the feelings at the time. If I had known, I would have done that for you."

"Because you understand my heart," she whispered.

"I think so, at least enough to know what scares you and what makes you happy. I know that the reason I had those terrible cravings for bear claws wasn't that I was addicted to pastries, but because my soul had to somehow convince my head of the truth."

"I missed you," she cried sadly. "I'm glad you started coming around again, even if I didn't want to admit it." Her crying turned into a yawn and her eyes nearly closed.

I sat up and twisted around, pulling her with me until we were both on the pillows and then I pulled the covers over us.

"What are you doing?" she asked.

I pulled her into me and smoothed the hair from her face before I kissed her lips chastely. "I'm going to sleep with you in my arms. You're exhausted." I smiled at her, but she frowned.

"But..."

I put my finger on her lips. "But nothing. We have all the time in the world to be together, and when we share that kind of intimacy, I want you to be fully awake and fully aware of how good I'm making you feel. Okay?"

She nodded and I reached over her and grabbed my phone off the table.

"What are you doing?" she asked, her brow pulled down to her nose.

I noticed a text from Dully and flipped the phone open, reading it.

"Everyone is as excited as you were. Thanks for the great advice. D."

"You're smiling. Why are you smiling?" she asked and I gave her the phone. She read the message and laughed softly. "That's so awesome."

"It is awesome, but do you know what I really wanted the phone for?" I took the phone from her hand and opened the camera, holding it up. "Say selfie," I whispered and for the first time, she actually said it, and the smile I captured was one I would never forget.

Chapter Seventeen

Liberty

I chuckled when a photo popped up on the small screen. It was Bram and me in front of Bubba Gump's Shrimp Co. where we had enjoyed a late lunch at the Mall of America. I flicked the photo to the left and straight out laughed at the next picture. He had snapped it just as I had my brace hooked around a pole. I was aiming for sexy, but I looked ridiculous.

His iPhone had become the way to watch our relationship unfold through pictures. The first one he took on his phone in the bakery, I looked stiff and uncomfortable, but today's pictures were different. I was different. I was in love.

The next picture to pop up was the selfie I took of us just as he kissed me. I'm pretty sure it was what you call an ace shot by an amateur, who couldn't stop laughing, while she took the picture.

When we woke up this morning, he told me he had arranged for Mark and Lucinda to work one more day, so we could stay in Minneapolis and enjoy some of the sights. He took me to breakfast and then to the Mall of America, where he patiently walked with me, no matter how slow I had to go. When we left the mall, he took me to the sculpture garden, and then when I was too tired to walk any more, we came back to the music lounge for a light dinner and drinks. I had showered and was resting now, while he took his turn in the bathroom.

"Whatcha doing?" he asked. He surprised me when he came out of the bathroom, still drying his hair. He was in nothing but one of the white robes from the hotel and a little part of me ached to see what was underneath.

I held the phone to my chest as the next picture came up. It was of us in the sculpture gardens with the spoonbridge and cherry as a backdrop. "I'm looking at pictures of us."

He laid the towel over his shoulder. "Is there a song called that?"

"It's actually called Pictures of You, but you were close," I laughed.

"I like pictures of you." He grinned at me and I shook the phone.

"I noticed. I found a few in here I didn't even know you took."

He came over and took the phone from me, then flipped through the album. "You mean like this one?"

He held up the phone and I looked closely. I was on the bleachers at the basketball game that night, holding Jo-Jo in my arms. He had taken the picture from above and I was gazing down at her, my finger on her cheek trying to calm her. It was in the instant he snapped the picture that she opened her eyes to look at me.

"She's such a sweetie. They're so lucky to have such adorable little girls," I said and he nodded.

He lowered himself to the bed. "Did you see this one?" he asked, holding up the phone. It was in his texts and sent by Dully.

I put my hand over my mouth when I saw it. Adam stood in the middle of all the other Alexanders, holding Jo-Jo and wearing a huge grin on his face under a sign that said *Welcome Home, Adam*. Sunny was holding a sign that said *Congratulations, Uncle Bram!*

"Oh, my goodness…" I said softly, in awe of the wonderfulness that was his family.

"Pretty great, right?" he asked and I nodded because I couldn't speak.

"The text says, we missed you at dinner and Adam wondered why there was no Miss Liberty to sit next to. How about if you make sure you're both here next week? We'll even let you take an official Alexander family picture. It's about time for a new one.'"

He lowered the phone and set it on the table. "Why are you crying, babe?"

"Because your family is so great, and I'm so happy for Adam," I tried to explain as I swiped at my tears. That was only part of the reason, but I wasn't going to tell him all of it.

He pulled a tissue out of the box on the desk

and brought it over. I took it from him and dabbed at my eyes. "Thanks, sorry for being so emotional." I took a shaky breath.

"I'm very happy for Adam, too, but I think there's more to it than that. I think you see something in that picture you wish you had, but don't think you can ever have it again. Maybe, you even think you don't deserve to have it again."

I closed my eyes to shut him out more than anything. "Let's watch a movie, Bram. I need to rest."

His hand squeezed my thigh firmly until I opened my eyes. "When you were in the restroom at the mall today, my mom called. She wanted to check on you, and make sure I was treating you right."

"What did you tell her?"

"I told her that you were good and we were having fun and to leave us alone," he laughed.

"Bram, be nice to your mom," I teased.

"Then, when you were in the shower, Snow called me. She wanted a report on how your leg was and how you were feeling."

"She's very sweet, and a good doctor." I leaned up against the headboard to get more comfortable.

"Yeah, she is, and I'm pretty sure the only reason she didn't insist on talking to you was because we will be home tomorrow." He raised his brow and shook my foot a little.

"What do you want me to say, Bram?" I asked, resigned.

"I don't want you to say anything, but I do want you to be honest with yourself about how you're feeling."

"You want me to say aloud that I covet the time I spend with your family, but I feel guilty about it because my own family is dead? There, I said it. Happy?" I asked and crossed my arms over my chest.

He shook his head. "No, that doesn't make me happy. It makes me sad, but yes, I did want you to say it. Saying it releases the hold it has on you. My parents always told us that, and over the years, I've learned they were right." He held up the picture again and I bit my lip. "You helped Dully remember that lesson last week and because of it, this happened. He remembered that saying it out loud would set him free of it, and once he did, he was able to see what his heart wanted him to do."

I balled the tissue up in my hand and he laid the phone down on the table next to the bed.

"You think that by saying that I feel guilty about wanting to be part of a family again, it will assuage my guilt and let me move on?" I asked and he nodded.

He brushed a wayward lock off my face. "I know a way you can test the theory out." He grinned and I shook my finger at him.

"Let me guess, go to family dinner with you next week?"

He leaned over and pressed me further into the bed, his body draping me like a blanket. "And the next week, and the next, and the next," he whispered as his lips came closer and closer to mine.

"Just kiss me," I sighed and he did, his lips warm from the shower. His bare chest heated my insides as he lay on my breasts, which were bare beneath the nightshirt I was wearing.

He trailed kisses down my neck and sucked gently where my pulse beat rapidly. "Do you feel what you do to me, Liberty Belle?" he moaned as he rubbed himself against me, so I could feel his hardness.

I slipped my hand between us and brushed his need, taken aback when the bathrobe parted and my hand caressed his velvety skin. I noticed his breathing change to short bursts, mimicking the same rhythm my hand did.

"You're so soft," I whispered in amazement, my lack of experience rearing its head as he laughed into my neck. It was erotic and a shiver raced down my spine.

"It might be the only part of me that's soft, but you, on the other hand," he paused long enough to slip his hand under the nightshirt and massage my breast, "are soft everywhere, and I want more."

He lifted himself off me long enough to sit back and pull the nightshirt over my head, making bare all the soft parts of me he wanted to touch. His robe was still open, and when he cupped my breasts, I noticed him bob with desire.

"Will you make me feel good?" I whispered and he lowered himself over me again, his tongue coming out to trace my nipple in a wet trail. I moaned when he did the same to the other side.

"Does that feel good?" he asked, then blew on the wet spot until it was dry. From my vantage point, I could see my nipple pointed toward the ceiling in desire.

"Yes, yes, that feels good," I cried out.

He continued his torture on my breasts and slipped his hand lower to part my legs. His fingers caressed the slickness that waited for him and he moaned.

"Oh, Liberty, you're going to be the one to make me feel good. Better than good, you're going to take away my breath and leave me dying to follow you anywhere," he groaned.

His mouth left my breasts to search out my lips. I held his face to mine and looked him in the eye, the fear in mine not something I could hide. "Because you understand my heart?"

"And because you understand mine."

His tongue pushed its way inside my mouth, and his actions left no question in my mind exactly what he wanted to do to my body. With his soft tongue and smooth hands, he brought me to a level of arousal I had never experienced before.

"I love you, Liberty. Can you feel how much?" he asked as he trailed kisses down to my breasts. I nodded my head slowly. "Do you love me, too?"

"Yes, I love you, Bram," I cried, grinding my hips into his. "I need relief from the pressure building in me. Please." I begged softly.

"Then come with me, my love, into the field and be mine," he said right before he claimed my lips again.

Chapter Eighteen

Bram

"Hi, how you doing?" I asked, sitting down on the blanket next to her. We finished dinner a while ago and now Liberty was stretched out on a blanket with Lila Jo.

"I'm doing okay," she answered and leaned her head against my shoulder. "I'm just feeling weak and tired today for some reason."

"You've had a busy few weeks with weddings and not much downtime. Snow said it's to be expected when you first start the meds. Some days will be worse than others."

"You talked to Snow about me?"

I tweaked her nose once. "Yes, while we did the dishes. I talked to her because I love you and I was worried about you. I wondered if I should take you home."

"No, please don't. I'm happy right here in the sunshine and the warm air," she said quickly.

"You tell me when and I'll take you, but don't stay and tire yourself out if you need to rest." I looked at her under one brow.

She held one hand up. "Okay, I won't, but I

think little Miss Jo-Jo is about to fall asleep, so maybe we will both stretch out and catch a few summertime winks."

I ran my finger down my niece's cheek as she rested on my girlfriend's shoulder, both reclined in a safe, supported position. "I love the way you look with a baby in your arms."

She closed her eyes and swallowed hard. "Bram."

"Liberty," I teased.

"I don't know if it will ever be safe for me to be a mother. Not to mention, do I want to put my kids at risk of getting MS?"

I started searching around the yard and pond with my hand to my forehead to block the sun.

"What are you doing?" she asked haughtily.

"I'm looking for Snow."

"She's up at the house. You know that."

I turned to her and laid my hand on the baby's back. "I do know that which tells me she isn't the least bit concerned about her two-month-old being unsafe in your arms."

"Not the same, Bram," she jumped in.

"It's kinda the same, Lib. I understand your fears. I've seen it with Snow, and I've seen it with Jay. Being a disabled mom takes a little more planning for Snow, but that baby and Sunny are always safe.

"Do you think I'm disabled?" she asked sharply.

"I didn't say that. I said disabled mom meaning Snow, not you."

"But that's what you meant," she pointed out, sounding resigned.

"Liberty, I won't downplay your fears about how MS will affect your life going forward. I would never do that. I'm just trying to show you that making solid decisions now is a waste of time. I can completely understand not wanting to pass on a gene for a disease that has so deeply affected your family. All you can do is get the test and find out if you have the gene. If you do have it, then you re-evaluate and think about what you want to do. I'm looking at you right now, though, and I can tell the kind of mom you would be."

"Me too," Snow said from behind us and I turned quickly.

"Hi, Snow, I didn't hear you coming."

She patted the wheels of the chair. "I added stealth mode to Mac, so I can sneak up on people."

I had to chuckle at the look on Liberty's face and Snow flat out laughed.

"I'm kidding, Liberty. Actually, you were just too lost in conversation to notice me. I thought I should check on Jo-Jo," she explained.

"See, Bram, I told you, so not mother material," Liberty said sarcastically, and Snow cleared her throat.

"Ahh, I didn't say anything about you not being capable of taking care of Jo-Jo. I was simply checking on my daughter, but since she's asleep on your shoulder, I'll be on my way," Snow said, a little taken aback. She started to roll her wheelchair down toward the pond where Sunny was playing with Jay.

"Snow, I'm sorry. I wasn't saying you were. You just interrupted a conversation we were having," Liberty apologized while she motioned between us.

Snow stopped the chair and turned it halfway toward us. "I know what conversation you were having. I've had it with Dully, and Jay will, or has, had it with December. Look at Sunny. Does she look damaged in any way?" Snow asked, pointing toward the little girl frolicking in the water.

"Of course not," Liberty whispered.

"Of course not, and she has a disabled mom in a wheelchair. You're too young to play the pity party game, Liberty. No two able-bodied women take care of their children the same way, just like Jay won't take care of his kids the same way I take care of mine. It's not about inability, it's about abilities, and you have plenty. The contentment of that ten-pound baby on your chest is proof of that." She turned back around and rolled toward Sunny, who waved excitedly when she caught sight of her mom.

"Guess she told me," Liberty frowned. She focused on the baby's head, so she didn't have to look at me.

"Snow doesn't mince words and she doesn't say things that aren't true. She also gives damn good advice." I tentatively stroked her leg and she gazed at me suspiciously.

"What are you doing?"

"I'm rubbing your leg to help you relax and go to sleep," I answered.

I knew her current attitude had everything to do with exhaustion and nothing to do with how she really felt inside.

"Like you would a child," she snapped and I bit the inside of my lip for a moment.

"No, like I would a twenty-five-year-old baker who needs to relax a little bit and get some sleep, so she feels better."

"I can't sleep, I need to make sure the baby is safe," she said, not making eye contact.

I rose up on my knees and moved behind her, adjusting her, the pillow, and the baby until they were both resting on my chest. I put my arms around her, one hand on the baby and one on her hand, resting on her belly.

"We will keep her safe together. Now, sleep," I commanded.

I couldn't see her face, but I could hear her tears even as she tried to hide them.

Liberty

I stood at the edge of the line of Alexanders: Tom and Suzie, Dully's family and Adam, Jake and his family, Mandy and her two kids, Jay and December, and since they insisted I was family, I waited for Bram to finish setting up the camera so he could join me. When I woke up from a short nap, I felt much better and wasn't snapping at people like the turtle in the pond. *Sleep or snap* would have to be my motto for a while, I guess.

"Okay, everybody on the count of three say selfie!" Bram yelled, running to stand behind me. He leaned over my shoulder and everyone was laughing as the camera snapped multiple pictures in succession.

He ran back over to check them out and then declared he had the perfect serious family picture.

"Now, we need a silly one," he proclaimed, fiddling with his camera. "Everybody on the count of three, kiss your partner!" Bram shouted, again running toward me.

Everyone turned to look at him just as he dipped me then planted a kiss square on my lips. The camera whirred and then the air was filled with full-on laughter as everyone pointed at us. We were the only ones kissing.

Bram stood me back on my feet and kissed me again for good measure then ran back to the camera. He bent over at the waist, laughing at whatever he saw there.

He gave everyone two thumbs-up and the crowd dispersed back to the pond. I sat down on Sunny's blanket, and Dully tenderly lifted Snow from her chair. He set her by me, then took the baby from Suzie, and handed her to Snow. Adam sat next to Snow and Dully passed Sunny off to Uncle Jay, so he could get a much-needed break.

Adam leaned around Snow to talk to me. "Wasn't that fun, Miss Liberty? We're part of the family now!"

I laughed with him, watching Snow's heart melt at his words. "It sure was, Adam. Though, I'm slightly embarrassed by that rascally Bram and his antics." I winked and pretended to be embarrassed.

"Don't be embarrassed, Miss Liberty, he loves you."

"You think so?" I asked, feigning shock.

"I know he does because he acts the same as Mr. Dully does toward Ms. Snow." He nodded that his statement was the most profound.

Snow tapped him on the leg. "What did we talk about when we told you that you are family now, Adam? Do you remember?"

He grinned and nodded. "Sorry, I forgot, Snow."

"That's okay, Adam, I know you called Dully that for a lot of years," she said encouragingly, and he nodded.

"He was my teacher for," he paused and counted on his fingers, "six years." He hung his head and clapped his hands together a few times.

"What's the matter, Adam?" Dully asked, laying a hand on the boy's shoulder.

Adam gazed up at the man he worshipped. "Do you remember how sad I was when they told me I had to go to the big kid school?" Adam asked and Dully nodded. "That's because I knew I would miss you so much."

Dully kept a steady hand on his shoulder. "I know, buddy, but that's why I promised to be your Big Brother, remember?"

Adam smiled sadly. "I'm glad you always came to help me with my Boy Scouts. It's hard not having a dad. My dad didn't want me because of my Down Syndrome. He said I would never be smart or be able to learn anything. I wish you were my dad, Dully."

Snow handed me Jo-Jo in one motion and took the boy by his shoulders. He was twice her size, but she was always bigger than life. "Your dad was wrong, Adam. You're very smart and a sweet young man. He's the one who's missing out."

Dully ruffled Adam's hair. "My beautiful wife is right. He's missing out, and I'm the lucky one. I get to do those dad things with you like Boy Scouts and ball games."

Adam glanced between the two of them. "Would it be okay if I call you dad? Or maybe Dully Dad? I might like to call you Mom if that's okay, Snow, I miss calling someone Mom," Adam said, his face hopeful, but hesitant, while he waited.

Dully kissed Snow's hand and winked at her. "I think Mom and Dad would be perfect, son."

Adam let out a whoop of joy and then grabbed them both while yelling, "Group hug!"

By the time he finished squishing them, they were all laughing. I jiggled the baby over my shoulder until Snow could take her back to nurse her.

Dully squeezed Adam's shoulder. "I talked with the school last week and got everything changed so you can ride to school with me when it starts this fall. We will have to go in and meet with Ms. Lake about your work program, too."

"Work program?" I asked Adam, and he glanced at Dully.

"Answer her question, Adam. I'll help if you can't remember."

"I remember all of it, Dad!" Adam beamed at the use of the word. "I'm old enough now to apply for the work program at school. That's where they match us with places in the community that can teach us job skills. That way, when I graduate, I have a skill I can use to get a job," he explained proudly, his chest puffed out.

"I see. That's a really great program, Adam. Where are you going to work?" I asked. I hugged my knees and made conversation while Sunny squealed from the pond, and I waited for Bram to come back.

"I don't know, but I hope it's with food. I really like cooking," he answered honestly.

"I've noticed you have some great skills in the kitchen with Suzie. I watched you measure, mix, and bake the cake this morning," I pointed out and if possible, he beamed even brighter. I turned to Dully. "You know, I have that big old bakery and I sure could use more help. Could he work for me?"

Dully sat up a little straighter. "I'm not sure, but I don't see why not. The Liberty Belle is a legitimate business and part of the Chamber of Commerce."

I turned back to the boy. "Adam, I'm a master baker, do you know what that means?"

He nodded. "Being a master means you're really good at something. Dad calls me the Uno Master."

I laughed freely for the first time in a long time. "Exactly, it means you're really, really good at something. For me, I'm really good at baking and making cakes. Do you know what it means to be an apprentice?"

He pointed his finger out toward the lawn. "Yes, it's when Donald Trump yells, *you're fired!*"

I fell over onto the blanket and laughed until I couldn't breathe. Snow's laughter was audible through the yard, too, and it took me a minute to pull myself together. I gave Adam a high five.

"You're right, that show is called *The Apprentice*. However, in the bakery, I won't be yelling, you're fired," I joked. "Being an apprentice in the bakery means you learn all the important steps to make buns, bread, donuts, and cake."

He gazed at Dully. "Do you think I'm smart enough to do that?"

Dully squeezed his shoulder and lowered his brow. "Adam, we've talked about this. You're very smart. You can do anything you set your mind to."

I felt like I needed to reassure him, too. "Adam, can you count to twelve?"

He glanced up at me quickly, "Of course, Miss

Liberty. I can count to one thousand."

I laughed a little and gave him a thumbs-up. "That's great, Adam, but in the bakery, all you need to know is how to count to twelve because we do everything by the dozen," I explained and he shook his head no.

"No, you don't. You do everything by a baker's dozen. You always sent thirteen donuts home with mom."

I chuckled. "Okay, you got me there. When it comes to donuts, it's always a baker's dozen, but when it's buns or rolls, it's always twelve. Those are the kinds of things you learn as an apprentice."

"Would I be an apprentice forever?" he asked.

"No, after you do what they call an apprenticeship, then you become a journeyman. When you're a journeyman baker, you learn more advanced techniques for decorating cakes and things like that. There is always something to learn or try in a bakery, and usually, they are always pretty tasty," I teased.

Dully spoke up next. "I'm a little worried about his schedule and the dangers that are in a bakery."

I thought about it for a moment. "I agree, Dully. There are a lot of dangerous pieces of equipment to deal with. That's easy to work around, though. To start, he would just be a bench helper, where he picks the buns from the wheel and puts them on the pans in rows of twelve, or pans the bread before it goes in the oven. Mark and I would do all the mixing, and using the ovens and fryers. If he could start this summer, maybe a few mornings a week, we could teach him how to be a bench hand in no time. Then once school starts, if he comes in whenever they release him, the equipment will be cool and he can help me clean it. I can take the time needed to explain how all the machines work. This summer, he can also work in the front of the house and learn how we package and take orders. If he's still interested after all of that, he can start working one weekend morning and we will progress him through the equipment. I'm assuming there's a job coach who might help us with planning those things?"

"Yes, that's why we will have to meet with Ms. Lake next week. She likes to have it all set up, so they can have their orientation done during the summer. What do you think, Adam? Would you like to work at the Liberty Belle?" Dully asked.

"I really, really would, Miss Liberty!"

"Looks like I should come to that meeting with Ms. Lake then?" I asked and both Adam and Dully nodded, Adam a little more vigorously.

"She will be so proud that I already have a job offer, Mom." Adam hugged Snow and she patted his back, even though she was still nursing Jo.

"She will be, Adam, and I think you're pretty lucky to get to work in one of the oldest businesses in Snowberry. Not to mention, she sells your most favorite food ever," Snow laughed lightly.

"Donuts!" he exclaimed and I gave him another high five.

I hugged my knees again and thought about all the things I could teach him. "Maybe one of the first things you can do is create a new donut for the bakery case. If the customers like it, we can make it an official donut for the Liberty Belle, and you get to name it," I told him, excited for the first time in a long time about bakery work.

"That would be so cool, Miss Liberty!" He clapped again and his face was lit up like the Fourth of July.

I held my finger up. "Okay, but this is contingent on just one thing."

Adam looked at Dully, "Contingent? What does contingent mean?"

Dully told him how to spell it so he could look it up on his phone. Adam read the definition and then looked up at me.

"What is the job contingent on, Miss Liberty?" he asked properly.

"Excellent use of the word in a sentence, Adam. The contingency is that you stop calling me Miss Liberty and just call me Liberty or even Lib is fine, deal?" I asked, holding out my hand and he pumped it up and down multiple times.

"Deal!"

Chapter Nineteen

"You've got it, Adam. Just keep bagging them like I showed you," I told the boy who was getting the day-old bread and buns put together for the nursing home. "I'll be right back. I have to go check the cooler for a cake."

"Okay, Lib. Thank you." He smiled sweetly, his enthusiasm for the job reminding me I could make an impact in the community with more than just my bakery goods.

I went to the cooler and pulled it open. I had to search for the cake Mark told me he made earlier this morning amongst all the extra stock he had prepped for the weekend. The cake was a special-order carrot cake for a wedding on Saturday. I found the cake, and the two dozen cupcakes, in a box labeled *Nickerson Wedding*.

I stared at them, trying to work out in my mind how I would decorate and arrange the heavy cakes. When an order for a tiered carrot cake comes in, it's always a trick to find a creative way to display them, due to the weight of the cake and the icing. Thankfully, the wedding was indoors, or it would be impossible to keep the frosting from sliding off the cake.

I stepped out of the cooler and closed it behind me. I laid out some parchment paper on the bench, intent on drawing the design while Adam was up front taking care of customers. When I met with him, Dully, and Ms. Lake, the very day following our great idea, Ms. Lake was ecstatic. She was thrilled that I wanted to be part of the work program, and even more thrilled that I was willing to train Adam without a job coach here every second of every day. I just didn't feel it was necessary. He may have special needs, but he was smart and learned things easily when presented the right way. I had no doubt we could manage the majority of his work duties without any outside help.

Today was his third day working with me, and he quickly surprised me with his passion for the job. He told me he always thought he would never be able to have a skilled job because no one would give him a chance to try. He was determined to do the very best job he could. This week he learned how to make change for a dollar, five dollars and ten dollars as well as how to pack thirteen donuts into a box, so they fit without the frosting being smashed.

The stairs Bram and Dully made were getting a work out since Adam wasn't much taller than I was. He was fantastic with the customers with his bubbly personality, and I'd seen faces I hadn't seen in a long time stopping by to wish him well.

I heard yelling from the front of the bakery and

dropped my pen. What on earth was going on? I hurried around the wall and stopped in my tracks when I saw Winifred at the counter.

"I will not talk to someone like you," she sneered in Adam's face.

"By someone like him, you mean a teenager, right?" I asked, coming to his rescue. She turned her nose up a little and waved her hand at him as though he would, or should, disappear.

"What can we do for you, Winifred?" I asked. I held Adam in place next to me while we waited for her answer.

"I need to order a cake for the library for next week," she spat.

"We will be happy to take your order," I assured her, then turned to Adam.

"When someone wants to order a cake, do you remember what pad we use?" I asked and he held it up, having already written Winifred - Library on the top. He may not have gotten all the right information, but I wouldn't have to guess whom the cake was for.

"I was just asking her what kind of cake she wanted, but she didn't want to tell me," he explained.

I turned back to Winifred. "Is that so? Well, why don't you ask her again, Adam?" I instructed without taking my eyes off the wicked woman in front of me.

Adam asked her again what kind of cake she wanted using the polite way I taught him. Winifred reluctantly gave him the details of the cake, which he wrote down, a little too slow for her taste, however. The look of disdain on her face was bringing my blood pressure up and she needed to leave before I exploded. When Adam finished the order, he went down the stairs to lay it in the back where I keep the special orders.

Winifred huffed from in front of the counter. "I cannot believe you employ people like that."

I went around the counter and put my hand on my hip. "By people like that, are you referring to my apprentice?"

She laughed snidely. "That's your apprentice? Wow, this place is really going downhill. I heard you were struggling to manage this place by yourself."

I kept the smile plastered on my face, even though I wanted to punch her in the throat. "It was nice to see you again, Winifred. I'll have the cake ready for you to pick up by nine," I paused as I ushered her out the door. "On second thought, I'll deliver it to the library at nine. Have a nice day."

I closed the bakery door as soon as she was through, locked it, and shook my head in frustration. That woman has been nothing but a pain in my backside since she moved into her parents' house after they died. I would have rather she sold it and not polluted Snowberry with her venom. I glanced up and Adam stood at the bakery case with a resigned look on his face.

"Just ignore her, Adam. She's a real sourpuss.

She's mean to everyone," I promised.

"I heard what she said, Lib," he said quietly and untied his apron. "Maybe I shouldn't work here."

I marched over and kept his hands from removing the apron. "No, Adam, that's just Winifred. She was icky because you're a teenager." I tried to blow it off, but he wouldn't budge. He held his ground in the silent room.

"No, she meant the R-word," he insisted. "I hear it all the time. The kids at school think we're too dumb to know what retard means, but we aren't. We know. When the teachers tell them they can't use that word anymore, they think up a new one. Why do people not give us a chance? Am I doing a bad job in the bakery?" he asked sadly.

I took his arm and led him to the back, so he could sit on my stool. I leaned on the bench with my elbows and sighed. "Adam, you're doing a great job here and you've only been working for three days." I pointed toward the front of the bakery. "You didn't need me out there to take Winifred's order. I know that. Has anyone else given you a hard time the past few days?"

He shook his head after he thought about it for a bit. "Everyone has been excited to see me here!"

I smiled and nodded encouragingly. "That's because most of the people in this town are loving, wonderful people who are excited to see their friends working at the places they love to frequent. Winifred isn't one of those people, but we just have to smile and help her, and people like her, the best we can. Do you understand what I mean?"

He shrugged. "I guess. You mean like when Dully tells me I have to be nice to my teacher even though she's not him, and I really want him to be my teacher?" he asked and I laughed in agreement.

"Yes, exactly like that, Adam. Will you help me make the best cake the library has ever seen and then deliver it with me? We have to have it there by nine next Monday, so you'll have to be here early."

He stood up and did a jaunty salute, which made me laugh lightly, and my shoulders relaxed. "Yes, Liberty, I will make you proud."

I took his hand down from his head and gave him a hug. "You already have made me proud, Adam. You know what? The door is locked and we have nothing left to do. I say we work on that special donut we talked about."

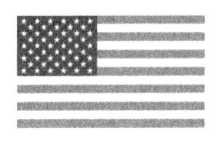

Bram

The sun was starting to set by the time I stopped at Liberty's house. I was afraid she was in bed because she wasn't answering my texts, but I was nervous in general for some unexplained reason. I told myself I would just see if any lights were on and if all was quiet, I would check on her in the morning. The part of me that kept saying she should at least be responding to my texts made my hand knock on her door. There was a light shining from the kitchen, which ramped up my nervousness. If she was home, why wasn't she responding?

The screen door shook a little as she opened the door and I sighed in relief. She stood before me in shorts and a t-shirt, her hands held up, sporting a pair of rubber gloves like a surgeon. She motioned me in with them and I pulled open the screen door.

"Hi, Bram. Did I forget a date or something?" she asked, going back to the sink where there was a can of scouring powder and a piece of steel wool.

"No, but you didn't answer my texts and I was worried," I explained. I stood transfixed as she started scrubbing the bottom of the sink again as though it was a boat with a bad case of barnacles.

"Can't text with these gloves on. I was going to respond when I finished. How was your day?" she asked without looking up, her concentration intense on the white powder that filled the sink.

"My day was fine. I caught a few tuna fish out on Snowberry Lake and then asked people to take pictures with them on the lakewalk," I fibbed.

"That's cool," she grunted. She turned the water on to rinse away the white mess with her gloved hands.

I stepped closer to her and hit the faucet handle until the water turned off, and she finally looked at me.

"For God's sake, you're going to scour the finish

right off this sink. I just told you I caught tuna fish in Snowberry Lake and you said, *cool*. What's going on?" I heard my tone and knew it was cross, but the woman obviously had a problem.

"Nothing's going on, so I wasn't paying attention. Excuse me." She wrenched her arm out of my hand and took her gloves off, throwing them into the sink. She tried to take a step around me and cried out, nearly falling to the floor.

I grabbed her, but her right leg was held away from her body and it was shaking. She was gasping for air and her eyes were squeezed closed, her face twisted in pain. I carried her to the couch the best I could and laid her down, pulling at her shorts to get to the Velcro that held the brace on around her waist. I had to get the brace off her leg.

"It's okay, Liberty. Just take some deep breaths," I encouraged her calmly, but she panted like a woman in labor. I finally loosened the Velcro and pulled the brace off.

Her leg was in some sort of spasm with her calf knotted in a tight ball. Her foot was pulled down as soon as it was free of the brace, and she cried out again. I grabbed her leg to massage it the best I could, and trapped my phone under my ear. I waited while it rang, and the adrenaline left me rocking with each ring.

"Hey, Bram, what's happening so late?" Snow asked when she answered.

"I'm with Liberty and something is wrong. Her whole leg is in a Charlie horse, I think? I'm not really sure, but she can hardly breathe. What do I do? Should I take her to the ER?" I asked frantically while my hands squeezed and kneaded her foot and calf.

"Bram, stay calm, this is very common in MS. You need to massage the muscles until they start to loosen up, can you do that?" Snow asked. I nodded then remembered I needed to speak.

"Yes, that's what I'm doing," I answered.

I snuck a look at Liberty's face and it was locked in a painful grimace and tears streamed down her face.

"Keep doing that until you start to feel it release under your hands. Is it her whole leg or just the calf?" Snow asked.

"Her calf and foot. It's like the arch is pulling her toes down," I explained the best I could.

"Okay, she probably forgot a dose of her medication. Is the massage helping?" Snow asked as though this was any other day at the office.

I let out a relieved sigh. "Yes, it doesn't seem as tight. Her toes aren't as rigid either." I took one hand off her leg to brush the hair off her face. "It's okay, Lib. Try to take a couple of deep breaths."

I watched her force herself to respond to my words and her chest rose once and then fell.

"Is she panting? I don't want her to pass out," Snow said, concerned.

"She was, but the cramp seems to have lessened and she's not in as much pain," I said, relieved.

I heard shuffling in the background and then Snow spoke again. "Here's what I want you to do, Bram. Ask her if she took her baclofen today."

"Snow needs to know if you took your baclofen, Liberty," I said very authoritatively and she shook her head.

"I forgot," she said, her voice winded and filled with pain.

"She says she forgot. Should I have her take it?" I asked Snow.

"Yes, make sure she only takes the one dose, though. Don't double up because she forgot one. See if she has a heating pad and wrap it around the calf to keep the muscle warm. After the baclofen has thirty minutes or so to work, she should be able to walk again. If she can't, then I will meet you at the ER."

"Okay, I can do that," I assured her.

"I think you should stay with her tonight, Bram. Adam said she got really upset at work today about a customer, but he couldn't, or wouldn't, say anything more than that. I suspect something was said about him working there," Snow confided. "Has she been acting weird tonight?"

I laughed and glanced at her yellow gloves, still visible from where I sat. "Well, when I got here, she was trying to scrub the finish off the sink."

Snow chuckled, but I could tell she was upset by what Adam did and didn't tell her. "That might indicate a problem. Go easy on her, but see if you can get to the bottom of what happened. Call me if you need anything else, Bram."

I assured her I would and she hung up on her end. I let the phone fall to the couch rather than take my hands off Liberty's leg.

"Take some slow, deep breaths, Lib. Tell me where I can find your medication. Snow wants you to take it. She says in half an hour, you'll feel better." I kissed her forehead while I waited for her to answer me.

"By the sink in that pillbox," she said weakly. "Can you get the heating pad in my bedroom? That usually helps."

I kissed her again and nodded. "I'll be right back."

I jogged to her room and unplugged the heating pad that she was using a lot more than she let on, obviously. I reached over and grabbed the pillbox on my way to the fridge and searched through it for a drink. I found a water bottle and carried the whole lot to the coffee table. I plugged the heating pad in and wrapped it around her calf, the cramp better, but not gone. I didn't know what pills she needed, so I handed her the box then held out the bottle of water. She looked in the box and paused as though she was unsure of what to do.

"Snow said if you missed a dose not to take two, just take one dose now and start over tomorrow."

She rested her palm against her forehead for a second. "Sorry, I forgot to take it earlier and I'm not used to it enough yet to know how to make up for that," she said, putting a pill in her mouth and taking the bottle from me. She washed it down and rubbed a hand over her face. "I'm sorry you had to see that. I'm usually able to control them, but that one was bad."

"Don't apologize, Lib. You get cramps like that a lot?"

She shrugged. "Yeah, but not usually that bad. The medication has helped."

"Why did you forget to take it?" I asked, and she glanced at the clock on the wall.

"I lost track of time. Is it really after eight already?"

I nodded, then brushed another hair off her face. "It is. I've been texting you since six when I was at the game. I was worried about you, so I left the game and came over. Why were you scrubbing the sink like a madwoman?"

"It was dirty. So was the tub and the floor," she said sarcastically.

"You've spent the whole night cleaning?" I deduced and she touched her nose to say bingo.

She laid her head back and I watched her start to relax as the heating pad took the pain away. I kept massaging her arch, thankful when the muscle was flaccid under my fingers.

"Did you have a bad day at work?" I asked. I wanted to give her an opening to talk about whatever may have happened.

"That might be an understatement. The last customer of the day was Wicked Winifred." At the mention of the woman's name, she grimaced.

I groaned. "That woman needs to carry a warning sign when she walks into a place. What was her latest problem?" I pulled her hand to my lips then kissed it to show her I loved her.

"She wanted to order a cake, but she didn't want Adam to take her order. Said she couldn't believe I had people like that working for me," she relayed sadly. "I didn't give her a choice, though. I forced her to tell Adam what she wanted and he took her order just fine. When he went in the back to put the order where I keep them ..." she sighed and waved her hand at me. "Never mind. I just don't like her. She is way too surly for someone her age."

I took the hand she was flipping around and held it still. "No, not never mind. Tell me what she did."

"She said she heard I was having a hard time running the place by myself, and it must be the truth if I was employing those kinds of people," she whispered.

"And by those kinds of people, she meant?" I paused purposely to let the question hang in the air.

She shook her head when tears gathered in the lids. "Adam says she meant the R-word. I tried to tell him that wasn't true, but he proceeded to lecture me that he knows people call him that all the time, and he's used to it. I can't believe someone has to get used to being called such derogatory names," she sniffed.

"How did Adam react? Snow said he wouldn't tell her."

"He agreed to help me make the cake, decorate it, and go with me Monday to deliver it." She smiled, and I gave her a low high five.

"That's my boy. He won't let her get away with treating him poorly. He never does, and he manages to do it with a smile on his face and nothing but love in his heart."

She nodded at my words. "I know."

I held her hand. "So that only leaves one thing you can be upset about."

She turned on her side to face away from me. "I'm tired. I should get some sleep before I have to go back to work in the morning."

My hand kept a steady rhythm on her belly. "I'm going to stay tonight. Snow thought that was a good idea. I'm also going to call Mark and have him come in tomorrow morning to get things started, so you can sleep in."

As expected, she sat straight up and stuck her finger in my face before my words were finished. "I do not need you to stay here, and I do not need you sticking your nose in my business!" she yelled, right in my face.

I didn't react to her anger and forced my face to remain calm. "Instead, you're going to run yourself into the ground just to prove to Wicked Winifred that you can run the place yourself? You know she doesn't actually care, right? She just says those things because she's mean and vindictive."

She lay back on the pillow and I watched her neck bob up and down as she swallowed back the tears that were threatening to fall. "She's right, though, Bram. I can't run the place by myself anymore. I've tried for the last three years, but I'm so tired."

"I know, sweetheart. Everyone can see how tired you are. What I can't figure out is, why you think you have to do it all yourself?" I tucked her hair behind her ears and watched her face contort through a range of emotions.

"That bakery is my dad's legacy, Bram. It's the place where he lived, but more importantly, it's the place where he died. I can't let him down. He always said he put his heart and soul into it for me. I don't want to let him down."

"I can understand that, Lib, but he wouldn't want you to hurt yourself, either. He wouldn't want you to start hating the work because you can't keep up the pace you've set for yourself," I tried to soothe, but she jumped in.

"He did it. He spent his whole career there," she countered and I held up my finger.

"That's true, but he also had help. He had your mom who ran the front of the house, and you as a bench hand. He had several other apprentices and journeymen I remember over the years. When he was alive, you didn't have MS. What would he be doing if he was alive and knew you were sick?" I asked and waited for her to think it over.

She laughed a little. "I remember when Mom used to have a relapse. He would fret over her nonstop until she was better. He wouldn't let her work. He always called in a neighbor, or church lady, and paid them under the table in pies and cakes."

I tickled her belly with my fingers that rested over her belly button. "Exactly, and you know he would be doing the same thing if he was here and you were sick." She nodded and I kissed her lips gently. "Besides, in my opinion, there are a lot of ways to look at Winifred's comment. She says she heard you couldn't take care of the place, but she's wrong. When you saw that you were starting to sink physically, you did what any shrewd business person would do. You brought in people who could do the job you needed them to do in order to keep things running smoothly. You're an excellent baker and businesswoman. You know what has to happen and you get the job done. Delegating responsibilities is an important thing to learn, and your dad taught you that very well. You just forgot in your busyness how to remember."

A small smile tipped her lips. "I guess I didn't think of it that way."

"Good thing I'm around." I winked and she laughed for the first time since I got there.

"Good thing. My leg feels much better, thank you for helping. I was so angry about what happened. I let her nasty words put me in danger." She held her hand to her forehead and groaned.

"We're all human, Lib. Our emotions get the

best of us all the time. When you nearly fell down, the only emotion that controlled me was fear. Everything I did for the next five minutes was spurred by that one emotion. Snow broke through it and helped me remember to feel the other emotions, like love. I won't sit here and tell you that you have to love Winifred, but you understand what I mean."

She lowered her hand to her lap. "I do understand. I'm sorry I scared you. Will you help me shower? I feel like it would be a good idea if you are near when I'm in there." She shrugged and I turned the heating pad off and laid it on the floor.

I picked her up and held her in my arms, pressing a kiss to her lips before I started toward the bathroom. "I'll get you started in the shower and while you're washing, I'll call Mark then get your bed ready."

I lowered her to the shower chair and helped her pull her shirt off and unhooked her bra before I turned to give her some privacy.

"You've seen it all before, Bram," she whispered.

I nodded with my back still turned. "I have, but tonight you need rest, not me ravishing your body."

"Who says we can't do both?" she asked, and I turned back toward her. She pulled the curtain closed slowly, her lips pulled up in that sexy grin I had come to love.

Chapter Twenty

Liberty

"You're always so gentle, Bram. How do you keep such tight self-control?" My head rested on his bare chest and he ran his hand up and down my back lightly.

He sighed and his hand stopped its motions on my back. "It's not tight self-control. It's love. I love you and I will do anything to keep from hurting you. Anything. I've never understood the idea of inflicting pain during lovemaking. That's the time you should feel nothing but pleasure."

"I love you too, Bram. I guess I've never really thought about pain being an erotic lead-in to lovemaking. I don't think I would find it nearly as erotic as I find your gentleness." I was so comfortable I was almost asleep in his arms after our lovemaking. "I don't want you to leave. Can you stay tonight?" I trailed my fingers through his fine blond chest hair.

"I'm not getting out of this bed until it's time to take you into work. Mark will be in to start the donuts and I'll take you in to get your cake together before the wedding. We're working the same one, so I'll help you do set up before I start pictures."

His hand picked up the rhythm on my back again and I nodded against his chest, losing my fight against a yawn. I closed my eyes just for a second to rest them while my mind played his words like a melodious tune. He loves me and he would never hurt me...

I heard him calling my name, "Liberty. Liberty, wake up, sweetheart."

"Bram, I'm not asleep yet. We just made love," I sighed, snuggling deeper into his chest.

He chuckled in my ear. "It's almost five, babe. We've been asleep for hours," he assured me.

I opened my eyes and squinted at the digital clock next to the bed. Indeed, it read four-fifty a.m.

I held my face in my hands for a moment. "I guess that pill made me tired. I'm going to need coffee to get through today."

He leaned me back on the pillow and rolled over to pin me under him. "We have ten minutes. I can think of something that will wake you up better than coffee."

"Oh, really? I'm not sure I want to find out what can be done in only ten minutes," I whispered. I tried to stretch and wiggle a little under him.

He started to kiss my neck, his breath warm on my skin until he made it to my earlobe where he blew sharply and goosebumps rose across my entire body. "The first minute, I'll use my lips to wake up your skin," he whispered in my ear before those lips kissed lower to where my tank top ended and my breasts began. He didn't let the small amount of fabric stop him. Instead, he tugged at my nipple through the material until I could feel the moistness from his tongue.

He held my hands over my head and kissed his way down to my belly, where he blew across it again, watching as the bumps grew on my skin. "The second minute, I'm going to use to take these annoying clothes off you, so I can wake up other parts of you with my warm hands."

He pulled the shirt off in one motion and my shorts off in another. I lay bare and his hands were on me immediately. He massaged my breasts for a moment until he couldn't resist and covered one with his lips again. His free hand slid lower, between my thighs, and I couldn't bite back the moan any longer.

He fondled my thighs, a hiss escaping his lips when he felt the triangle between them. "I see I won't have to work too hard on waking up that part," he moaned, his lips off my nipple and back to my neck.

He kissed his way to my lips and then took possession of them, matching the rhythm of the kiss to the rhythm of his hand. I gasped against his lips, trying to get the breath that my lungs screamed for, but also trying not to end the party before it began.

I grabbed his hand and held it still. "I'm going

to embarrass myself," I moaned, and he laughed the naughty laugh he reserves for only the bedroom.

"Only men do that, babe. Bringing a woman to pleasure more than once in ten minutes is what every man aims for, and I have seven minutes left."

He grinned at me in the low light of the room and started the rhythm again, waiting for me to close my eyes and trust him. I was so close I could feel the waves as they built inside me. My brain was foggy and wanted to forget about the bed and the room, and just be off in the darkness in that instant euphoria. I tensed when his hand slowed just a fraction. He pulled off his own clothes and took protection from the nightstand. He knelt between my legs and pushed my thighs apart further with his knees. I was too far gone to care.

"I love you, Bram," I called out into the darkness. The first wave of pleasure forced the words from my mouth.

He paused at my entrance, his hands holding my arms over my head before he plunged inside me, right between the waves that consumed me. His heat made my breath hitch, but as he moved inside me, it drew out the pleasure so much I just went higher. I thrashed under him as he made love to me. His hips rocked me with each thrust and his need was spurred by the way my body reacted to his.

"I love how you feel, Liberty. I can't hang on," he cried, and his hips stilled as he gave in to the moment that our love created.

I kissed his cheek as he lay on top of me, his face pressed into my neck while his body spasmed. "I love you, Bram, so much," I whispered in his ear.

He rose up on his elbows to gaze at me. "I love you so much I couldn't even make it ten minutes." He grinned sheepishly, and I kissed him tenderly.

"True, but you did aim high and hit the mark, so you should be happy about that," I teased, as he rolled off me.

"I'll be happy when I get to be the one to hold you every night," he said and then grimaced a little. He swallowed nervously. "Sorry, that sounded overbearing and possessive."

I ran my hand down his bare chest. "Not really. It sounded like you love me and don't want to live without me. I can get behind that. It's been a long time since I've felt this loved, and I don't mean just sexually. I mean emotionally in the way you make me feel on a day-to-day basis. Like last night, when you didn't run away because I was an idiot and forgot to take my meds, but instead did everything you could to make me feel better."

He trapped my hand on his chest. "You're not an idiot and I would never run away. It broke my heart to see you in so much pain. I don't want to see you in pain, so I would do anything to make it go away."

I looked down at his hand over mine and back up to his face, the morning stubble making him look older than his twenty-some years. "Do you think you can keep loving me even when things aren't easy? Do you think you can keep loving me when I can't do the things you can, or when I can't give you the family you want?" He closed his eyes and shook his head just a little, but enough for me to see. He brought my hand to his lips to kiss but didn't speak. "Bram, when you answer, please look at me. I have to see your eyes to know if it's the truth," I begged.

"I'm not looking at you because I can't stand to see the pain in your eyes when you ask those questions."

"The answer is no, right? I understand, Bram. I know you think I don't, but I do," I tried to say, but he was shaking me by my arms.

"Stop. Just stop, right now," he hissed. He let go of me long enough to turn the lamp on next to the bed. "I turned that lamp on so you can see my face when I answer your question. If you can't believe my words, then you sure as hell are going to believe the truth you see in my eyes. Can I keep loving you when things get hard? The answer is yes. When you love someone, you don't stop just because life isn't always paradise. You fight, together, until things get easier, and you learn to appreciate the good times a lot more. Can I keep loving you when you can't do the things I can? Does that mean like when I can play baseball and you can't, or I can go hiking and you can't?" he asked sharply and waited, so I nodded, feeling diminutive under his gaze. "The answer is yes, I can keep loving you then, too. I don't expect you to play baseball, you hate it. I know even that little detail about you. If you want to go hiking and can't, I'll find a way for you to go, even if I carry you on my back. That's what you do when you love someone." He trailed his finger down my cheek, his eyes telling me everything his words didn't.

My chin trembled until he cupped it in his palm. "I had to be sure, Bram."

He kissed me then, scooting closer until his knees touched mine and his hands were wrapped up in my hair. When we both needed air, he pulled back slowly but kept his hands where they were. "You know my family, Lib. You know that when we fall in love with someone, there are no circumstances that are going to keep us from being with that person, ever. Even if one of those circumstances is that we can't have a family."

I froze in place, his words a reminder that he didn't forget about the last question I had asked. Here it comes, the reason he won't stay. I know his family, and I know how he adores his nieces and nephews. As much as he thinks he loves me, he will always resent me for that part of it.

"If the MS wasn't in the picture, would you want kids, Lib?" he asked and I nodded without making eye contact.

"But the MS is in the picture and I don't want to pass along something to them that I could otherwise prevent," I explained.

He lifted my chin with his finger. "And I completely understand that, babe. I know Snow has talked to you a little bit about this, but there is no real way to test for the genes like I thought there was. Not yet, anyway. She also told me that even if you carry the gene and we had a child, our baby would only have a 50/50 chance of getting it, because no one in my immediate family has MS. Along with that goes the knowledge that if you did pass a gene to one of our children, something in the environment would still have to trigger it. Something that triggered yours may not trigger theirs. Are you following me?"

I nodded. "I know this, Bram, I just…"

"I know all of this is very new to you and you don't know how *to just feel* about any of it. I want to be clear that I would never push you into having children if it's not something you can live with," he soothed.

"I want to have a family. I don't like being alone in this world. I want to have a warm little baby to hold and love like Lila Jo. I want to have a little girl like Sunny, who laughs with delight at the new cake I make her. I want to have a boy like Adam who is wonderful in so many different ways. I know that it doesn't make a lot of sense that on the one hand, I want to desperately not have a baby, and on the other hand, I so desperately do."

"Maybe it seems to you like it doesn't make a lot of sense, but it makes total sense to me. Here's the thing, babe. We can have a family. Maybe they won't be biologically ours, but there are a lot of kids out there who need homes. Adam is the perfect example. Families don't have to be made from our genes. They can be made from nothing more than our love," he promised.

"You would do that? If I said no to getting pregnant?" I just wanted to be sure what I heard him say was what he really felt.

"In a heartbeat, Lib. You would never see someone move so fast to make an appointment with an adoption agency. Here's the thing, we have a lot of time to think about those things. We're young and we have a lot of living and loving of each other to do before we worry about bringing anyone else into our lives. Okay?" he asked and I nodded.

"Okay. I feel better. Thank you for always listening to my fears and not downplaying them."

He kissed my lips and then my forehead. "I told you before that I would never do that, Lib. We all have fears. I have a fear, and that's losing you after I've waited so long to be with you. I just remind myself that I have found the one my soul loves."

"You have, so have I," I promised. My resolve and belief were much deeper than a few moments ago.

He ran his hand over my thigh and sighed. "I know we are being responsible and using condoms, but if we want to be sure you don't get pregnant, I think we need to do something a little bit more effective. Condoms can break, and I would never want to put you in the position of having to make a choice you don't want to make."

I held his hand to my cheek. "I started taking the pill when I got the diagnosis. Snow asked me point-blank if I wanted it. We weren't active yet, but I wanted to be responsible. In another week or so, we won't need to worry about using condoms anymore, unless you want to, of course."

He kissed me then. His lips demanded my attention and his hands held my face tightly to his. "I love you for doing that and it puts my heart at ease, as I'm sure it does yours. I don't want to keep using condoms. I hate them. They keep me from being one with you in a way I so desperately need to be. They keep me from giving my whole self to you the way I so desperately want to. When that day arrives, please tell me. I promise it will be the day that you no longer wonder about any of the things your heart makes you wonder about right now. I will show you with my body how much my soul needs you."

I clung to him, his body chilled from sitting naked in the early morning air. He kissed my neck and uncurled his legs before sliding off the bed.

"Right now, we have a wedding to attend, my lady. I'm going to go clean up and get ready while you stretch out your legs, so they don't lock up, okay?" he asked and I nodded. He climbed off the bed and walked to the door of the bedroom, turning back around for a second. "Hey, Lib?" I glanced up at him and waited. "What are you doing for your birthday this year?"

I laughed at the odd question. "The same thing

I always do, nothing."

"You do nothing on your birthday? It's July Fourth."

I gave him the palms up. "Sometimes Lucinda and I go out drinking and to the fireworks, but alcohol and these medications don't mix. Besides, she'll be off with her boyfriend in Rochester this year."

He walked back to the bed and leaned his hands on the mattress. "Good thing, because you'll be busy with your boyfriend at Snowberry Lake this year."

"It sounds like a date," I whispered, my heart light in my chest.

Chapter Twenty-One

"I don't know about this, Liberty," Adam said nervously as we sat in the van outside the library. "Maybe I should wait out here. I don't want Winifred to get angry with you. Snow said you got real upset and got hurt the last time."

I sighed. "I did get upset, Adam, but it wasn't because Winifred doesn't like you working for me. I don't care what she thinks anyway, do you?"

"Dad told me a long time ago when people are mean to you, you should kill them with kindness," he spouted.

I laughed while I gave him a high five. "Dully is right, and you have learned how to do that very well. Let's go give them the cake and then we can drop off the pies at Noel's on the way back to the bakery, okay?" I asked and he jumped out of the van and threw the side door open to pull out the large sheet cake.

I held the door open for him and he proudly carried it through and right up to the circulation desk where he stood before Wicked Winifred. "The Liberty Belle with your cake, ma'am," Adam said professionally. I had to stifle a snicker at his ridiculously cute voice.

Winifred looked up disdainfully and waved her hand toward the back. "Just take it back there."

I moved in and held Adam in place. "Would you care to use your manners, Winifred? Adam was polite."

She stood up and leaned on the desk, making Adam take a step back. "I don't need to use manners with him, or you, for that matter. We are paying you for a service. End of story. Now take the cake to the back like I told you to."

My eyebrows went up to my hairline and I shook my head at the beautiful young woman in front of me. What was her problem? Didn't her parents teach her about decorum and proper etiquette?

"Is that so?" I asked, and she nodded her head once, as though she was dismissing us with her attitude. "We will be on our way then. Seeing as how you haven't paid us for the cake, I still own it. Let's go, Adam."

I calmly walked to the door and held it open for Adam to carry the cake through. He looked nervous, but I smiled as though it was any other day at the bakery. "No worries, Adam, just put the cake in the van," I assured him and pulled the van door open. He laid it in the back again and looked at the library door.

"But Liberty, they need a cake," he almost whined. He was near tears. I was about to explain it to him when the library door flew open and Ashley came running out, at least the best she could in heels and a pencil skirt.

"Liberty! Liberty, don't go," she puffed, working her way down to the van.

Ashley was the head librarian and one of my favorite ladies in town. She didn't have a mean bone in her body and spent the majority of her time helping the schools find funding for library books.

"I'm so sorry, Liberty. I saw the exchange, but couldn't hear what was said." She motioned toward the library in agitation.

"Winifred can't seem to find her manners this morning, Ms. Ashley," Adam said. His voice was still filled with anxiety and his hands twisted around in front of him. "I think I made her mad, and then Liberty really made her mad. I don't like it when people are mad."

Ashley put her arm around his shoulder and tried to calm him. "No one is mad, Adam. Winifred is just difficult, and you're right, sometimes she can't find her manners. I appreciate that you used yours with her despite the fact that she couldn't show you the same respect."

"Yes, ma'am." He smiled then and I was relieved I wouldn't have to call Dully to diffuse the situation.

Ashley shook her finger a little at Adam. "Say, I got a call from Patrick not that long ago about a new donut he tried down at the Belle this morning. You know anything about that?" she asked Adam, and his smile got even bigger.

"Was it shaped like an A?" he asked and she nodded. "That was the new donut I made! I used an A because my name is Adam and now, I live with the Alexanders. Liberty fried them, but I got to glaze them and put the nuts and sprinkles on."

"Is that so? Well, Patrick said he got the last one, but he sure hopes you make more because he likes a donut with a little bit of cinnamon, a whole lot of glaze, and even more peanuts," she chuckled at her husband's love for the dough, though I noticed it was strained.

"They're all gone?" Adam asked, aghast. "We made twenty-four of them. That's two dozen, Liberty."

I held my hand up and he gave me a high five. "I think we have a winner, Adam. We'll make three dozen tomorrow. Do you know how many that is?" I asked and he paused to add twelve to twenty-four.

"That's thirty-six Amazing A donuts!" he laughed, and Ashley and I did, too.

"Maybe you should make a few dozen for the library tomorrow, too. I'll be in to get them before we open. Make sure you make me one that has extra glaze and lots of sprinkles," Ashley ordered and Adam opened the van door and pulled out an order form.

"I'll make a special order, so we don't forget," he promised very seriously.

Ashley turned to me and pulled me aside. "I'm sorry about Winifred. I've heard she's causing havoc all over town. I'm sure if she was this impolite today, she wasn't much better when she ordered the cake."

"Worse," I mumbled and she grimaced.

"Listen, let's take the cake in the back and I'll pay you from petty cash. I don't know what we are going to do with that woman, but I've about had enough of her."

I smiled, not sure what to say. "I'll get the cake."

"Maybe someone should get her a dog," Adam said from the front of the van, and I turned to stare at him.

"What's that?" I asked him.

"It seems like Winifred needs someone to love, and if she forgets to use her manners with a dog, it would never know and just keep loving on her," he explained logically.

Ashley covered her laughter with her hand. "I love that boy. He really thinks things through."

It was late, nearly six, and I was still at the bakery, but it was necessary with the holiday coming up. I had extra inventory to order, so I took advantage of the peace and quiet after closing to get it done. The bakery would only be open a few hours on the morning of the Fourth. Just long enough for people to pick up their orders, for the locals to get their buns for their cookouts, and the campers their donuts when they struggled into town. Then I was shutting it down and spending the day with my boyfriend and his family. Bram planned to come over after his softball game tonight, so I still had a few hours before he would expect me to be home.

There was a knock on the door and glanced up from the counter where I was stocking tissues and bags. Snow was sitting there with Jo-Jo on her chest in a carrier, waving at me. I hurried to the door and unlocked it, letting her in.

"Hey, Snow, what has you out so late this fine evening?" I asked, relocking the door behind her.

"I was supposed to be having dinner with my husband, but he got called to a fire. Before I went home, I thought I would stop in and say hi," she explained.

Dully and Bram were both volunteer firefighters for the Snowberry Department. Our town was too small to have a fully staffed department.

"Did Bram get called in, too?" I asked and she shrugged.

"I don't know. Dully just kissed me and took off like a shot," she said, patting Jo's back.

I pulled out a chair and sat down in front of her. "Well, since it's after six and I'm not usually here, I find it hard to believe you just thought you would stop by to say hello."

She snickered and her smile told me I had called her on her fib. "You got me there. I saw you working on my way back to the van and wanted to check on you. How are you feeling?"

I patted my right leg and tried to look hopeful. "I feel better. My leg hasn't improved much, but the strength in my hand has. I can decorate longer before it gets tired."

"That's good. That means the medications are working to bring you out of the relapse. We talked about the fact that you may never recover a lot of strength in the leg, even if you aren't in a relapse," she reiterated and I nodded.

"I know, and I do okay with the brace as long as I'm smart and don't overdo it. Sorry Bram bothered you the other night. I was kind of out of it," I stuttered, and she laid her hand on my arm.

"No, you don't get to apologize for that. We're family, and believe me, I was dressed with my keys in my hand when he called me back to say you were okay. If Bram is going to be in your life, you're going to have to learn that it's somewhat of a package deal. You get Bram, but all the rest of us are there to support you both when you need it."

"He's made that pretty clear," I teased and she nodded.

"It took me about three or four family dinners when I first met Dully to really understand how quickly they accept someone into their family. I had been an orphan for a long time, only having Savannah to love and take care of me. It can be a little overwhelming in the beginning."

"I've known the Alexanders for a long time, but you're right, once they consider you one of theirs, they're like pit bulls protecting a bone. No one is getting near it."

She laughed long and relaxed, Jo stirring on her chest. "Oh, my, you do have them pegged. I need to use that analogy. Those Alexander boys can be pushy when they want to be. That leads me to my next question. Is Bram being pushy? I mean like physically. Is he respecting you and being careful?"

I raised a brow and coughed once. "Excuse me?" I asked quietly.

She glanced up at me and then held up her hand, sitting up straighter in her chair.

"Oh, that came out all wrong. I didn't mean it like that. I meant like physically when you need help. That he doesn't push you to do things you can't physically do just because he wants to do them," she explained, obviously flustered.

I leaned back against the chair and tried to calm my heart. "He's very respectful and careful. We talked about it and we know what we both want from a relationship. We had that talk you said we would someday have, and he understands how I feel about having kids right now."

"Good, I tried to answer his questions without being disrespectful to you and taking into consideration the way you would feel about him talking to me without your knowledge. You might as well know that every Alexander boy does it when they're worried about the woman they love. Dully asked his dad straight out one day if he should have a vasectomy, so he didn't put me at risk if I got pregnant," she chuckled and shook her head.

"Does having a baby put you at risk?" I asked, surprised, and she laughed harder.

"No, that's just it. I have no problems other than I can't walk and I need to take extra calcium for my bones, but he was convinced that carrying a baby would be dangerous for me. His dad set him straight, as you can see." She smiled at the little girl who was holding her finger tightly.

"I just need some time to see how this is going to play out. It hasn't been long enough for us to know anything, and I don't want him to be disappointed if I can't give him children. He says he won't be, but I feel that in a family like the Alexanders, he will be."

"Because we all love having kids and being part of a big noisy family?" she asked and I nodded. "It's true, we do love kids, but we don't much care how they come to us. Look at Adam. He's blossomed since he's come to live with us. He just needed a dad who could teach him all the important things in life that he was missing all these years. Speaking of Adam, he told me about the Amazing A donuts."

I laughed, and nodded, grateful the conversation had changed directions. "Ah, yes, the Amazing A's. Top sellers around here, that's for sure. Don't tell Adam, but I'm taking the money from the sales of those donuts and starting an account for him. If he keeps working here, he will have enough to buy his own set of cake decorating supplies and other baker's tools he will need as a journeyman. If he moves on to something else, I'll give him the money as a gift," I explained.

"What?" she asked, stunned. "You're already paying him minimum wage, which you shouldn't be since he's an apprentice, but that's …"

I bit my lip, nervous I had overstepped and tried to justify my reasons. "I know he could work here as an apprentice for nothing, but I don't work that way. He earns his wage and he will be paid accordingly. You and Dully are also on his checks, so you can control how the money is deposited. As for the other fund, I thought it was a good idea, but if you don't, I'll donate the money to the work program or something."

I forced myself to make eye contact with her and she had tears in her eyes. "No, you misunderstood me, Liberty. I meant that it's so sweet of you to do that for him. I can just imagine his face when he can go out and buy his own set of tools to use at his job. There are so many things he doesn't understand about life as an adult, but he's learning them now because you're willing to teach him. He always believed all he'd be able to do was scrub floors or wash dishes. He didn't think anyone would ever give him a chance to learn a trade that he enjoys. Adam is a smart boy, and people do him a disservice by always treating him as though he's not. Dully and I appreciate that you love him like we do."

I tried to give her a reassuring smile, but I had

tears threatening to spill over my lashes, too. "He's a good boy, Snow. He works hard and he brings an added benefit to this bakery ... positivity. I didn't realize how much I needed it until I noticed on the days we work together, I feel better. People are always trying to bring him down, but he's always lifting them up and they don't even know it. I think that deserves an extra layer of glaze and peanuts." I winked and she laughed, her head going up and down.

"Speaking of people bringing him down, what's this I hear from him about wanting to bring Winifred a dog?"

I threw my head back and laughed at the memory as I launched into my Wicked Winifred story.

Chapter Twenty-Two

Bram

My hands shook as I crawled into my SUV covered in soot and smoke. I held the phone in my sore, blackened hands and read the multiple texts Liberty sent since eight when I should have been at her place. It was nearly nine now and with each text, I could tell she was more and more worried. The last text was fifteen minutes ago and read, *"I talked to Snow and she said you're with Dully. Be safe."*

I set the phone on the seat and put the car in drive, pointing it toward her street. I wasn't sure of anything other than I needed to see her. I needed to be with her and feel her against me. Dully tried to get me to go home with him, but I couldn't. I had to see her. She would let me stay with her tonight, and she would let me hold her without knowing it was the only thing that would get me through the night.

The front porch light was on as I drew closer to the small ranch style home she had lived in all her life. It was comforting to know she was inside with her boy shorts on, and her hair pulled up in a ponytail away from her face.

I put the car in park and climbed out, acutely aware of the smell of acrid smoke I wore like bad cologne and the black soot that covered my clothes. I kicked my shoes off outside the door, startled by the whiteness of my socks in all the inky blackness I had just left. Before I could knock, she pulled the door open as though she knew I was standing there waiting for her to come to me. She held the door open and pulled me in, then looked me up and down.

"Bram?" she asked slowly.

I glanced up, the only part of me that was clean was my socks, but it didn't matter. I pulled her to me and held her so tightly I was afraid I was hurting her, but I couldn't let go.

"It's gone, Lib. It's all gone. All of it, just gone in the blink of an eye," I whispered, my eyes falling closed. The fatigue overwhelmed me as the adrenaline drained from my system.

She finally struggled free and I noticed the dirty soot smudges I left on her white t-shirt. I brushed at them with my hand but left even more smudges from my dirty, black fingers.

"I'm dirty. I've gotten you all dirty," I said sadly, and she pulled my face to hers.

"I can wash my shirt, Bram. Tell me what's happened. What's all gone?" she asked quickly. Somewhere in the back of my mind, it registered that my face hurt when she held it.

"My face hurts, Liberty. Please don't touch my

face," I begged and she dropped her hands instantly then steered me to a chair. I sat heavily and stared up at her. "You know my apartment?" I asked and she nodded. "It's gone, all of it. Both sides of the duplex burned right to the ground, and we couldn't do a damn thing to stop it."

She wrapped her arms around my shoulders. "I'm so sorry, honey. I don't know what to say other than I love you and I'm here for you."

She held my elbow and led me to her bathroom. She took the shower chair out and then she pulled my shirt, jeans, boxers, and socks off. She moved me into the shower and laid a towel on the chair outside it.

"You need to take a shower. Your face doesn't look burned, but use cool water and make sure you're careful when you wash, so you don't hurt the skin. I'll put your clothes in the washing machine and find something for you to wear," she ordered.

When I didn't move, she turned the faucet on and adjusted the water before she turned the sprayer on and handed me the soap. The water was a shock and I snapped forward, grabbing the soap from her hand. "Can you do this, or do you want help?" she asked.

"I'm good," I answered, pulling the curtain closed.

I turned the water a little more toward cold, letting it cool off my overheated skin from the blaze. The firefighter's gear is heavy and hot when it's not July, much less when it is. I know it wasn't smart to take my gear off and go back into the cooling cinder, but my entire life was strewn in that mess of water and soot. It took Dully's strong arms to remind me that the parts of my life that lay burned were only material things.

My apartment might be gone, but Dully was safe, and I had a beautiful woman waiting for me to come back to her safe and sound, too. I knew Dully would be over here as soon as he went home and told Snow about it. She would insist on coming here since I refused to go there. I couldn't. The only person who could offer me what I needed right now was Liberty.

I scrubbed at my skin and the black soot that covered it. I used half a bottle of shampoo trying to get the smell of smoke from my hair and by the time I shut the water off, it finally ran clear. I pulled the curtain aside and she sat waiting for me on the chair outside the tub. She held the fresh towel on her lap and stood up when I stepped out of the shower. She took the towel and dried me off, starting with my hair and my face, being tender and careful of the slight burn of my skin. She ran the towel down my arms to my hands, carefully drying the reddened skin on my palms. She moved lower, drying me as a mother would dry her child, with more love than I've experienced in a very long time. When she finished, she turned my palms over and looked up at me.

"Are those blisters?" she asked.

"Yeah, I touched some stuff when it was hot. I don't even remember. It's fine. They don't hurt," I promised.

She handed me a t-shirt and I slipped it over my head, then a pair of boxers and shorts. I looked down at my clothes.

"How did you get these?"

"You left them here one day after you had gone to the gym. I washed them and kept them in case you ever needed something to wear when you were here," she answered while she hung up the towel.

It all seemed so normal, a part of my everyday life, but tonight it was more like an illusion.

I pulled her to me and kissed her forehead. "It's all I have now, besides the clothes in the wash and the camera equipment I had in my SUV."

"No, you also have your family and me. Everything else can be replaced," she soothed. I followed her back to the kitchen and she pointed at the chair.

"Sit down and I'll get you a drink." She pulled a bottle of Jack down from the cupboard and poured me a shot. I kicked it back, thankful that the burn was something I was inflicting on myself and not something I couldn't control.

"I didn't think you drank hard liquor," I said when I could talk again.

She laughed and sat down by me. "I don't. That was my dad's secret stash. Hasn't been touched in three years."

I held the glass out and she filled it again then watched me hit it back. "Can I get you something to eat? You probably shouldn't drink on an empty stomach."

"She's not going to make it, Lib," I mumbled and she took the glass from my limp hand.

"What are you talking about?" she asked, lifting one brow.

"My neighbor, Mrs. Paul, was in the duplex when the fire started. By the time we got her out," I paused and tried to get my voice under control, but it was futile, "she was burned badly. We sent her to Rochester, but she won't make it."

She stood and pulled me up into her arms to hug me tightly. "I'm sorry, Bram. I don't even know what to say. This has nothing to do with your apartment and everything to do with you feeling guilty that you didn't get to her in time."

I nodded over her shoulder. "If I had been there, I could have gotten her out. I could have broken a window and gotten her out before the fire was too far gone."

She kept her hand moving on my back, soothing my ragged soul. She let me cry on her shoulder, and my shoulders shook as I thought about the horrible scene and how guilty I felt for not going home before the ballgame like I usually did.

I heard the door open and pulled away from her to see Dully and Snow in the front entrance. Dully had a plastic bag in his hand and Snow had her medical bag on her lap.

Liberty motioned them in. "Come in, guys."

"I got some of your spare clothes from Mom and Dad. I know you refused medical treatment at the scene, but now that you've seen Liberty, I'm hoping you'll let Snow look at your hands," Dully said, leading me toward the couch.

He sat me down and set the bag next to the couch. "I also stopped and picked up some new socks and boxers until you can drive into Rochester sometime in the next few days."

I glanced down at the clothes I was wearing. "Thank you. I appreciate it. I was lucky to have forgotten these here and Liberty washed them for me."

Snow rolled her chair over and rested her hands on my knees. I glanced at her and then back to Dully. "Did you hear any news? Is she going to make it?"

Dully shook his head a fraction of an inch to the negative and I sighed, the worst confirmed.

"She passed away in the helicopter before they got her to the hospital, Bram," Snow told me. "You did everything you could to help her, though. You have nothing to feel guilty about."

She turned my hands over and sighed, shaking her head at the blisters on my hands. "I really think you should go to the hospital, Bram. These need more treatment than I can give you here."

I shook my head sadly. "I'll go tomorrow. I can't do it tonight. I don't have it in me."

"Tomorrow is soon enough. Tonight, I'm going

to clean them the best I can with what I have in my bag; then cover them in silver ointment and wrap them," she explained, looking to Liberty. "Will you make sure he gets to the hospital tomorrow or do you need me to come get him?"

"I am not a child!" I exclaimed. "I'm in the room and I'm an adult. I have a car and I can drive it to the doctor to get my hands checked, Mommy."

Dully laid a hand on my shoulder and squeezed it. "She's just concerned about you, Bram."

Snow had her head down and was cleaning my hands as though I didn't exist in the room. "I'm sorry. I didn't mean to be a jerk. I'm not thinking clearly."

Snow glanced up and smiled at me. "It's okay. You're entitled to be a little bit of a jerk tonight. You've been through a lot. I don't want you to worry about anything, though. We will help you get through this and find you a new place to live."

I leaned my head back on the couch and sighed. "I will probably need to borrow first and last month's rent since I don't think I'm going to get my deposit back."

Dully bit back a laugh and Snow's shoulders shook as she tried to swallow her giggle. "I think we can swing it, bro. Just find a place and let us know."

"He can stay here," Liberty said from the chair where she had been watching the exchange. "I have this whole house to myself and it would be nice not to be alone. Don't worry, there are two bedrooms, so it's not like a moving in *moving in* kind of thing. He needs a place and I have one."

Snow finished wrapping my hands and the room was silent as her offer hung in the air. Snow moved her chair and I crawled over to Liberty and laid my head on her lap. "What if I want it to be a moving in *moving in* kind of thing?" I asked, desperately.

She brushed my hair with her fingers to calm me. "Why don't we talk about it tomorrow? You can stay tonight and tomorrow, when the sun comes up, we can figure all the rest out."

I nodded but didn't lift my head from her lap. Dully pushed Snow past the back of Liberty's recliner toward the door.

"We're going to go now. Get some rest, Bram, and we will check with you in the morning," Dully said, and as quickly as they showed up, they disappeared.

I glanced up at Liberty. "I want to go to bed. I want to hold you in my arms for the rest of the night and pretend this didn't happen. Can we do that?"

"We can, but only if you'll eat something first, and take some ibuprofen for your hands."

I stood and helped her up. "Okay, if it will make you happy, but I'm not hungry."

"It would make me feel better about leaving you early tomorrow morning," she said, going to the kitchen and fixing a sandwich.

She set it on the table with a glass of milk and

two pills. I resolved to eat it all just so she didn't look so worried.

"You've got a job to do, and so do I. I'll be fine. I'll go get my hands looked at and file my paperwork for the insurance. Then I'll go to work for what's left of the day." I took a bite of the sandwich and she massaged my shoulders, her hands warm, but tentative as she tried to comfort me the only way she knew how.

"I was going to open for a few hours the day after tomorrow, but I think I'll just do the delivery tomorrow morning for the café and bring them extra donuts for the out-of-towners and campers. It's the Fourth of July, so I'll keep the bakery closed and we can spend it together. Does that sound good?"

I turned around and smiled up at her. "It sounds perfect. I'll have to do some pictures for the paper with the fireworks and the events, but you can come with me or hang out with the rest of the family."

She kissed me and picked up my plate. "I think being a photographer's assistant might be kind of fun."

She walked by and I stood to grab her around the waist. I kissed her neck as I walked her into the bedroom.

"Oh, babe, I can make it more than kind of fun," I sighed.

Chapter Twenty-Three

Bram

I woke up alone. Her side of the bed was cold and I vaguely remembered when she had left me hours ago. My hands ached from last night as I sat on the edge of the bed and tried to wake up. My beautiful girlfriend had laid my clean clothes out on the bed that Dully had brought last night. I pulled the shirt over my head carefully so as not to aggravate my hands. My phone dinged and I smiled when I heard her text alert tone. Texting was going to be painful, but for her, it was worth it.

L: Hey, you up?
B: Just getting dressed. Was going to head down to file my insurance papers. What's up, buttercup?
L: I think you had better come down here.
B: To the bakery? Are you okay?

I shut the lights off to the room and took off for the front of the house where my shoes were.

L: I'm fine. Sorry to worry you. I'm at Kiss's Café.
B: You need help unloading or something? My hands hurt pretty badly.

L: No, just come down here, okay?
B: On my way.

I pulled the door closed behind me and made sure it locked then slipped into my shoes from yesterday. That was going to have to be the first stop for me after the café, new shoes. I climbed into the SUV and turned the engine over, checking the seat behind me, relieved to see all my camera equipment and computer. At least I didn't lose that in the fire. My heart flipped and I yanked the glove compartment open, heaving a sigh of relief when the box was still there. I took it out and stashed it in my computer bag, reminding myself to take it into the house tonight when I got back.

I drove toward the city center, wondering why Liberty wanted me to stop at the café. I wasn't hungry and she didn't need help, so I couldn't figure out the reason. My hands ached as I gripped the wheel and I prayed that I could get some relief before tomorrow when the paper needed me to take all the pictures for the parade and fireworks. My foot hesitated over the brake as I turned toward the café. Cars lined both sides of the street and I had to go around back to park. The parking lot there was full, too, so I parked on the street behind the café.

What is going on here? I jogged up the ramp at the front of the café and carefully pulled the door open. When I walked into the dining room, the place was utter chaos. My mom, Liberty, and Savannah stood watching it as though it was all perfectly normal.

"What on earth?" I whisper-asked and Savannah turned to me, surprised by the intrusion on their people watching.

"Bram! Good morning," she said happily, hugging me gently. Her little belly was quite obvious now and when she pulled away, I laid my hand on it.

"Good morning, Savannah. Look at you and this little belly," I teased and she laughed.

"This little guy is growing right on schedule, that's for sure."

"Little guy?"

"I think it's a boy, but we don't know for sure. Enough about me. How are you?" she asked and I glanced between her, Mom, and Liberty.

"I'm doing okay. I was just going to go to the clinic and then work. What's going on here?"

Mom hooked her arm in mine. "Everyone heard what happened and wanted to help, so they all decided to take over the café this morning to show support for you."

Liberty came over and kissed my cheek. "I have to get back to the bakery, but I love you. Stop over later? I'm closing at two."

I nodded and watched her work her way through the crowd toward the side door where her van was parked.

I heard my name called and turned to look at the lady coming toward me. With the mention of my name the whole room erupted and I knew instantly it was going to be a long time before I got to the clinic.

Liberty

"Are you sure you don't want me to open for a while tomorrow, Liberty? I don't mind," Mark assured me as he packed up to leave.

I put my arm around his shoulder and hugged him. "I'm sure, Mark. Thank you for helping me out so much right now. I think we all deserve a break and I'm going to take one, so should you."

He hugged me back and smiled fondly. "Your daddy would be so proud of you. You've kept this business open successfully after he died. He didn't even want you to be a baker."

I glanced up at him. "What?"

He grimaced a little as though he had said too much. "He told me once he hoped you did what you wanted to do, and not what you thought he wanted you to do."

"Ah, well, the good news is, I'm doing what I want to do. I've always loved baking and decorating cakes. I lost track of that for a little bit, but Bram helped me see that Dad wouldn't want me to do this alone and run myself into the ground physically," I explained.

"Bram is a smart guy. You should hang onto him. I'm glad I could finally retire and still have some life in these old bones to help you for a while. Have you thought about hiring a full-time baker?"

"I've thought about it, but I want to give Adam a chance. Does that sound like my head is in the clouds?" I asked, and he shook his head no.

"Not at all. I like Adam, and I've worked with some apprentices over the years that don't have half as much common sense and flexibility as he does. He's very quick on the draw with what we do here. Sure, he might have to write stuff down in his own way so he can remember it, but he always does things right. He has shown an excellent understanding of the sanitation and safety procedures for the equipment. I have no doubt he will be a journeyman in a year or less. Your dad would be really proud of the opportunity you're offering Adam, too. He always rooted for the underdog."

I hugged him again. "Thanks, Mark. Tell me if you get tired of working and want to enjoy real retirement. I don't want you to feel obligated to keep coming in to help."

He laughed as though I had just said the silliest thing ever. "My girl, I was retired for three whole months before you called me, and my wife was ready to ban me to the garage. I love having something to do and she loves having me out of the house for a bit every day. The extra money allows us the opportunity to do more things, so we all win. Besides, since Adam came to work with us, I've started to enjoy this job again. The last few years of my career, I felt the tedium weighing on me, but when Adam is around, work is fun. I enjoy teaching him the things I know about baking, and in turn, he always teaches me something about life in general. Win-win, my dear. Now, I'm going to get out of here so you can go home, too. Happy birthday, Liberty. I'll see you next week." He kissed my cheek and waved as he closed the heavy door behind him.

I smiled as I walked to the front of the bakery. I shut down the lights and checked the clock. It was after two already and I hadn't seen Bram since early this morning.

He had texted me a couple times with messages like, *"This is crazy"* and *"Can you rescue me?"*

I knew he was just kidding, but if I didn't hear from him again soon, I would hunt him down before I went home. I wanted to be sure he got his hands checked out before the holiday. His dad is a doctor, but delivering babies and dealing with burns are two completely different things.

A knock on the door snapped my head up and his face smiled back at me, his hand waving. I unlocked the door and pulled him in, so I could relock it behind him. I hugged him close to me, happy to see him after a long day.

"Hi, how are your hands?" I asked and he held them up for me to see.

"Better. The doctor put some special covering on them and gave me more to put on at home. He said to take it easy with them for the next few days. I might need a wagon to lug all my camera equipment around in tomorrow," he joked.

"Do you have to go in? Maybe they can have someone else do it?"

He smiled, kissing my hand as it caressed his cheek. "The guys at the paper tried to give me the rest of the week off, but they don't have anyone else who can do the job like I can. I'm not trying to sound like a bragger, but I'm really all they have in the photography department. I'll be okay as long as I get that photographer's assistant I was promised."

I nodded. "Of course, I'm looking forward to it. We'll get the job done together. What happened after I left the café this morning?"

He plopped down in a seat by the window. "Oh, my goodness, that was crazy." He shook his head over and over.

"Crazy like how?" I asked. I knew the reason everyone was there but wanted to hear his reaction to it.

"Crazy like *I can't believe all these people want to help m*e crazy," He rested his wrists on the table since his hands still hurt. "Mom said word got out before we had the fire out last night. The church ladies were already in Rochester at nine last night, getting the essentials I would need. My SUV is packed with new clothes, shoes, food, soaps, shampoo and …" he held up his hands, "you name it. Noel and Savannah agreed to have the café be a drop-off point for the community and wanted to donate all the proceeds from this morning's breakfast to me. Even the waitresses wanted to give me all their tips."

I rested my hand on his leg. "You didn't let them?"

He shook his head. "I couldn't do it, Liberty. Those girls count on that money to survive, and I'm okay. I have insurance that will cover most of what I need. I can't take from people who need it worse than I do."

"That had to be awkward, but I understand, Bram," I reassured him.

"It was, but I knew the girls were grateful when I refused. Noel and Savannah insisted, though. I took the money from them, and the money the people left in several well-placed jars in the café, and I'll make sure I do something right with it. I'll help Mrs. Paul's family first if they need it. The support alone would have been enough, but the donations were the cherry on top. Apparently, the church ladies texted my mom late into the night with pictures of clothes and shoes," he laughed, but I knew it was to cover the other emotions he was feeling. "I'm so thankful we live in a community like this that bands together during the tough times, and then tomorrow will come together again and celebrate."

"Me, too. I have experienced the same kind of love and support from the community lately, so I can understand how you're feeling."

He swallowed hard and nodded. "I still feel terrible about Mrs. Paul, but I know that I can't dwell on it, or I'll never get past it. It was her time to go," he sighed.

"Do they know the cause of the fire yet?"

"Unofficially, they think she may have fallen asleep with the stove on. It would explain why she didn't get out before being overcome with smoke."

I frowned. "She was starting to fail. Everyone in town saw it. I wish her family had, but I'm sure it's hard to tell someone they can't live independently anymore."

"That's the saddest part about it. She was supposed to be moving in with her daughter by the middle of this month. Life is so random."

"I couldn't agree more. I mean, look at my life. The first twenty-five years have been nothing but random. I need some predictability. Random is overrated."

He kissed me tenderly, close-lipped and soft. "Your life has been random, but also so beautiful, and our blessings are many." He stood and helped me up from the chair. "Can we go home?"

I gazed up at him and smiled. Home. He used the word as though my home had been his home for years rather than a day.

I took his hand in mine. "Yeah, let's go home."

Chapter Twenty-Four

Bram

"Liberty, wake up, baby," I called, shaking her shoulder.

She swatted at my hands and rolled away from me, snuggling under her blankets. "I don't have to go to work today," she mumbled.

I chuckled and ran my finger across her forehead then tapped her nose. "I know. Wake up, beautiful."

She opened her eyes and I was lying in front of her, my lips pulled up in a smile. She rose up and looked at the clock on the nightstand behind me. "It's only midnight," she moaned.

"I know that, too. I wanted to be the first to wish you a happy birthday. I love you, Liberty," I whispered right before I kissed her lips.

She returned my kiss. Her tongue warring with mine for position, but I won when she let hers fall and gave me full access. That hammer started ringing a bell in my head and I pulled away, my chest heaving.

"I want to make love to you, but we're out of protection. Promise me we'll get some more in the morning," I begged.

She held my face and kissed my lips. "We don't need condoms anymore. That's why I didn't buy any."

I closed my eyes and swallowed. She kept rubbing my face until I opened them again.

"What are you thinking?" she asked, and my heart thudded in my chest.

"How badly I want to make love with nothing between us for the first time, but how much trust that will take for you," I answered honestly.

She never moved off her pillow, but managed to strip herself of her tank top and shorts, her nipples erect the moment the cool air touched them. I bit back a moan and fought against touching her, my hand almost shaking as I held it back.

"Bram?" she asked and I forced my gaze to meet hers. "Is something wrong?"

"I want to make love to you so much …"

"I'm ready," she encouraged, holding her hand out to me. "It's my birthday, don't keep me waiting."

I nodded my head. "That's why I'm worried. It's your birthday, and I don't want to let you down. If I make love to you like this, I can't promise how long it will last. I've never had sex without a condom. More than that, I've never made love to the woman I want to spend the rest of my life with, without a condom."

She rolled to her side and I moaned when the dark circles on her breasts begged me to come to them. "You feel like this is our first time even though we've made love for months."

I nodded. "Stupid, I know, but that's how I feel."

She reached her hand out and laid it on my lap. "No, not stupid at all. I kind of feel the same way, honestly. I'm ready if you are, but if you want to wait, then we'll wait. I'm not worried about how much or how little time it takes. It will take however long it takes for our hearts, and our souls, to know if what we're feeling is real."

"I know what I'm feeling is real, but I need to show you," I whispered, taking her hand in mine. "I'm going to show you that all I'll ever need is you."

I bent my head and kissed her, my hand drawn to the breast that beckoned me with its firmness. She was warm under my touch, and her breath hitched in her throat when I rolled her nipple between my fingers. She moaned and flipped to her back, offering me complete access to her beautiful body, all of her laid out for me to touch. I knelt and grasped my shirt, careful of the bandages on my hands as I lifted it over my head. Her hand was massaging me through the shorts I wore and I pressed myself into her, letting her see and feel the power she had over me.

"Take them off," she ordered, and I raised a brow. "Now."

"Oh, Lib. I think some of my bossiness has worn off on you," I teased while I tossed the shorts behind me. She sat up and met my lips, my need for her pressing into her belly as we kissed each other hungrily, her lips sweet and her tongue hot against mine.

She forced me away from her lips. "I think you talk too much," she sighed, kissing her way down my belly until her lips surrounded my hardness. She tasted and teased me, her tongue swirling around my tip.

I gasped in pleasure and from the sweet pain I felt when she nipped at me, her hand coming back to rub away the pain until it was pure pleasure. I pushed her back, my resolve strained to the max.

"Stop doing that," I ordered, and she laughed naughtily.

"Now who's being pushy?" she asked, and I lay down on top of her.

"It's a trait of mine that you love, Liberty Belle." I breathed the words into her neck, feeling the goosebumps as they rose on her skin. "Tell me you love me," I begged, my body tense as I waited to hear the words.

"I love you, Bram Alexander, bossiness and all," she cried, arching her back to press closer to me.

Her invitation brought me to a fevered pitch, but I forced myself to wait. "What makes you most comfortable?" I asked and she smiled shyly, her face serene.

"Just like this. Show me your soul, Bram," she called, and I didn't hesitate.

I immersed myself in her slowly, and the feeling of perfection surrounded my entire body. My mind blurred as her heat encompassed me.

"That's perfect, right there," she said, raising her hips to mine. "Please, you feel so good, don't ever stop loving me," she called out, her hands in my hair.

I crushed my lips to hers at the same time my hips began to move on their own accord. "Never, Liberty, I love you too much. Do you feel the way I love you?" I asked and at that moment, she let go, calling my name softly. I couldn't do anything but the same, the spasm taking over before I could stop it. I filled her deeply, and my soul poured into hers until she had all of me, and I would never love another.

She wrapped her arms around me, her body limp, and I kissed her cheek. "I love you, my sweet birthday girl," I whispered.

"I love you so much. I don't ever want you to leave me."

I kissed her face again, my lips finding hers to reassure her the only way I could, while I was still buried inside her. "Never. I'll never leave you."

She relaxed then, her sigh of contentment music to my ears. I pulled away from her core and I sighed in defeat, hating the loss of her warmth and love.

"Sit up, babe," I encouraged, propping her against the headboard.

"Why?" she asked, her body still warm and relaxed.

"I want to ask you if your heart wonders anything."

She cocked her head and stared at me. "What do you mean?"

"Does it wonder if I love you?" I asked, and she shook her head no. "Does it wonder if I'll leave when the going gets tough?" I asked, and she shook her head again, but this time I saw the light come on.

She held my hand to her heart. "It doesn't wonder anything because it's filled with wonder at how much you love me, Bram. What we did there didn't feel like a physical act. It felt like a dance between our hearts, minds, and souls in a way I've never experienced before. Like we were both laid bare and only then could we really understand each other."

I smiled and caressed her warm breast tenderly. "That's exactly how I feel. I want to ask you a question." I waited and she nodded, making herself more comfortable against the headboard.

"Would it be okay with you if I moved in?"

"I'm confused. I already told you it was okay for you to live here," she reminded me and I nodded, taking her hand.

"I know you did, but what I mean is, I want to live here with you, forever." I leaned over her and turned on the small lamp, then opened the drawer in the nightstand and pulled out my shaving bag. I dug around in it until I found what I was after and handed it to her.

"I'm sitting here as stark naked as the day I

came into this world, and I'm asking you if you'll let me stay." I motioned to the bag in her hand.

She opened the small drawstring and pulled the wide gold ring out of the bag. Her hand shook when she brought it to her face in the low light of the room.

"I was going to ask you to marry me in front of my family tonight, but after what we shared together a few minutes ago, I want to ask you when we're the only ones here. Two souls, now one. Liberty, will you let me move in as your husband? Will you let me share the good times, so we can laugh and smile together? Will you let me share the hard times with you, so we can wipe each other's tears? Will you be the glaze on my donut in the morning and the butter on my bread in the evening? Will you be my wife?"

She cried silent tears as she held the ring up to the light. "Did you just ask me to marry you using bakery terms?" she giggled through her tears.

I kissed her, a little unsure of myself. "I wanted to be perfectly clear about what I want, babe. I want you, and I want you to be the one I always come home to."

She was staring so intently at the ring and not answering that I started to stutter, looking for ways to fill the silence. "That ring is the reason I didn't go home between work and the game the other night. I went to Rochester to pick it up and got the call on my way back into town. I had it custom made with a special coating that will protect it from all the work you do in the bakery."

She quickly held the ring out to me. "I can't keep this. You need to take it back and get your money back. It had to have cost a fortune."

I wrapped my hand around hers, the ring in my palm. "I can't take it back. They won't accept custom jewelry returns, and I don't need the money. I'm just fine with money. What I need is you, Lib," I practically begged.

I opened my palm and took the ring out of her fingers, holding it up. "When the jeweler asked what I wanted on the ring, I told him I wanted daisies because they remind me of spring, just like she does when she walks in a room. I wanted the diamonds in the center of each daisy to remind her that in our center is where our greatest gifts are, and as the daisy opens in the spring, it proudly displays its center for the world to see, just like you do. The thing is, I know you don't feel that way a lot of the time, so I got this ring for you. That way on a day when you're struggling with something, you can look down at the ring and remind yourself that I see your center, and it's what I love the most. That's why I want you to be my wife. I can't live without your center. Your beauty is breathtaking, but I know the one thing that will never change is your center."

She held her left hand to her chest and it was shaking in the light of the lamp. "You've taken me so much by surprise I've been rude. Ask me again?"

I laughed a little and took her hand from her

chest to hold in mine. "Liberty, will you marry me?"

I held the ring near her ring finger and she hadn't finished one nod before I slipped it on her finger.

"Yes, I'll marry you, Bram, for I have found the one my soul loves," she whispered.

My heart finally settled in my chest with her words.

I pulled her to me and held her close. "As has mine," I promised before I showed her just how much my soul loved her.

Epilogue

Liberty

September

The autumn sun was setting as we finished our picture session. My new husband directed the well-renowned photographer in the exact way he wanted the picture taken. I finally pulled him to me and kissed his lips to quiet him.

"You Alexander boys are so pushy," I teased, grabbing onto the lapels of his suit coat.

He spun me around and buried his face in my neck as we stood by a tree next to the pond in Dully's backyard.

"By the power vested in me by no one, I now pronounce you stuck with me for life," he said, his hands wrapped around my belly. I turned my face to gaze at him and kissed his lips.

"I don't think that's how it goes," I smirked. In one movement, he picked me up and then laid me down in the golden leaves under the tree.

"I follow my own rules," he teased. "I hope you don't mind being stuck with me forever. There are no refunds on custom men like me."

I laughed hysterically at the serious look on his face, as the photographer snapped away. "Custom man, huh? If you say so, dear."

He paused in his kisses along my neck. "Did you just call me dear?" he grunted.

"Yes, dear," I said again, and he commenced tickling until I couldn't breathe.

Just when I thought I would pass out from lack of breath, his lips settled over mine. I drew a breath instantly from the heat of his lips. He was my husband and I was his wife. We were one now, the way we should have been for years. His hand strayed to my hip and the photographer finally cleared his throat.

Bram ended the kiss abruptly and grinned sheepishly at me before he pulled me up and brushed off my dress.

"Why don't you two walk up the path and I'll get some shots in the waning sunlight," the photographer suggested.

Bram took my hand and swung it lightly as we walked to where our family waited. Our family, not just his. They loved me as much as I loved them, and without them, I would be lost. Since our engagement, Snow and Suzie spent countless hours with me planning the ceremony and reception. We wanted to keep it simple, so we chose a September wedding at the Alexander Family Farm, as I had come to call it, and that kept the cost and the planning time down.

Considering how busy I was at the bakery, and

how busy Bram was with photography jobs, we thought it might be December before we found a date that worked for both of us. I was so glad we didn't wait any longer, though. The weather was beautiful, and a real harvest sunset framed the minister as we said our vows.

Our family and friends lined the path that ran from Jay's cabin to Dully's driveway and they cheered and threw confetti as we walked past them toward the reception. I couldn't make it all the way and Bram stopped and pulled his phone from his pocket.

He held it up toward the sky and said, "Say selfie!" We both grinned at the camera when he hit the button. "Selfie!" I yelled loudly until a little girl came running at us.

She jumped into her uncle's arms and we repeated the process, making silly faces, even taking a selfie with the photographer who was laughing just as hard.

Bram knew I just needed a few minutes to recover and he managed to do it without making me look weak or sick.

I kissed him, whispering *thank you*, just as he snapped another picture that only we would ever see. He held out his arm to me and we made our way up the last few feet to the huge party tent that housed tables, chairs, and a buffet. Adam stood off to the end of the buffet table, his white baker's shirt pressed and clean as he stood at attention.

I ran to him and hugged him tightly. "Adam,

it's gorgeous." I clapped excitedly. The display of cake and cupcakes in front of him made me smile.

"Do you like it, Liberty? Mark and I worked really hard on them!" he exclaimed, a huge smile on his face.

"How could I not like them?" I asked, inspecting the cake closely. "I love them!" Joyful laughter escaped when I saw the cake topper. It was a bride and a groom kissing underneath a bell, the Liberty Bell. Red, white and blue streamers hung down from the cake like fireworks and the display of cupcakes on the table formed an American Flag. "You did an amazing job, Adam. You really have a flair for this. I'm very proud of you." I lavished praise on him as Bram stood behind me with his hand on my back.

The tent started to fill up with all the confetti throwers, and the DJ grabbed the microphone.

"Ladies and gentlemen, I give you Bram and Liberty Alexander!" he cheered, and the laughter and applause almost deafened us as we kissed. "As long as we have the bride and groom on the dance floor, we'll do things a little out of order and let them share their first dance while dinner is served."

A familiar tune from Cinderella began to play and I heard Sunny squeal when she recognized it.

"So, this is love," Bram grinned, wrapping his arms around my waist. "I think I could get used to this."

He twirled me around the floor carefully, my

brace unyielding to some of the trickier steps, but he made me look like a much better dancer than I was with his fancy moves. The music came to an end and everyone stood again, the applause loud inside the tent.

Bram held my face close to his, our foreheads touching. "Don't worry, babe, from this day forward you'll always be my belle of the ball."

The Snowberry Series

Snow Daze

Trapped in an elevator with a handsome stranger was the perfect meet-cute, but Dr. Snow Daze wasn't interested in being the heroine of any romance novel. A serious researcher at Providence Hospital in Snowberry, Minnesota, Snow doesn't have time for a personal life, which was exactly the way she liked it.

Dully Alexander hated elevators, until he was stuck in one with a beautiful snow angel. Intrigued by her gorgeous white hair, and her figure-hugging wheelchair, he knows he'll do anything to be her hero.

When a good old-fashioned Minnesota blizzard traps them at her apartment, he takes advantage of the crackling fire, whispered secrets on the couch, and stolen kisses in the night. Dully will stop at nothing to convince Snow she deserves her own happily ever after.

December Kiss

It's nearly Christmas in Snowberry Minnesota, but Jay Alexander is feeling anything but jolly. Stuck in the middle of town square with a flat tire on his worn-out wheelchair leaves him feeling grinchy.

December Kiss has only been in Snowberry for a few months when she happens upon this broken-down boy next door. His sandy brown hair and quirky smile has her hoisting his wheelchair into the back of her four horse Cherokee.

When a December romance blooms, Jay wants to give December just one thing for Christmas, her brother. Will Jay get his December Kiss under the mistletoe Christmas Eve?

Noel's Hart

Noel Kiss is a successful businessman, but adrift in his personal life. After he reconnects with his twin sister, Noel realizes he's bored, lonely, and searching for a change. That change might be waiting for him in Snowberry, Minnesota.

Savannah Hart is known in Snowberry as 'the smile maker' in Snowberry, Minnesota. She has poured blood, sweat, and tears into her flower emporium and loves spreading cheer throughout the community. She uses those colorful petals to hide her secrets from the people of Snowberry, but there's one man who can see right through them.

On December twenty-fourth, life changes for both Noel and Savannah. He finds a reason for change, and she finds the answer to a prayer. Desperate for relief, Savannah accepts Noel's crazy proposal, telling herself it will be easy to say goodbye when the time comes, but she's fooling no one.

Noel has until Valentine's Day to convince Savannah his arms are the shelter she's been yearning for. If he can't, the only thing he'll be holding on February 14th is a broken heart.

April Melody

April Melody loved her job as bookkeeper and hostess of Kiss's Café in Snowberry, Minnesota. What she didn't love was having to hide who she was on the inside, because of what people saw on the outside. April may not be able to hear them, but she could read the lies on their lips.

Martin Crow owns Crow's Hair and Nails, an upscale salon in the middle of bustling Snowberry. Crow hid from the world in the tiny town, and focused on helping women find their inner goddess. What he wasn't expecting to find was one of Snowberry's goddesses standing outside his apartment door.

Drawn together by their love of music, April and Crow discover guilt and hatred will steal their future. Together they learn to let love and forgiveness be the melody and harmony in their hearts.

Liberty Belle

Main Street is bustling in Snowberry, Minnesota, and nobody knows that better than the owner of the iconic bakery, the Liberty Belle. Handed the key to her namesake at barely twenty-one, Liberty has worked day and night to keep her parents' legacy alive. Now, three years later, she's a hotter mess than the batch of pies baking in her industrial-sized oven.

Photographer Bram Alexander has had his viewfinder focused on the heart of one woman since returning to Snowberry. For the last three years she's kept him at arm's length, but all bets are off when he finds her injured and alone on the bakery floor.

Liberty found falling in love with Bram easy, but convincing her tattered heart to trust him was much harder. Armed with small town determination and a heart of gold, Bram shows Liberty frame-by-frame how learning to trust him is as easy as pie.

Wicked Winifred

Winifred Papadopoulos, Freddie to her few friends, has a reputation in Snowberry, Minnesota. Behind her back, and occasionally to her face, she's known as Wicked Winifred. Freddie uses her sharp tongue as a defense mechanism to keep people at bay. The truth is, her heart was broken beyond repair at sixteen, and she doesn't intend to get close to anyone ever again. She didn't foresee a two-minute conversation at speed dating as the catalyst to turn her life upside down.

Flynn Steele didn't like dating. He liked speed dating even less. When his business partner insisted, he reluctantly agreed, sure it would be a waste of time, until he met the Wicked Witch of the West. He might not like dating, but the woman behind the green makeup intrigued him.

A downed power pole sets off a series of events neither Flynn nor Winifred saw coming. Their masks off, and their hearts open, they have until Halloween to decide if the scars of the past will bring them together or tear them apart. Grab your broomstick and hang on tight. This is going to be a bumpy ride...

Nick S. Klaus

Nick S. Klaus is a patient man, but living next door to Mandy Alexander for five years has him running low this Christmas season. He wants nothing more than to make her his Mrs. Klaus, but she'd rather pretend he isn't real.

Mandy Alexander is a single mom and full-time teacher. She doesn't have time to date or for the entanglements it can cause. Even if she did have time, getting involved with her next-door neighbor, and co-worker, Nick S. Klaus, had disaster written all over it.

This Christmas, Nick's determined to teach Mandy that love doesn't have to be complicated, and he's got two of the cutest Christmas elves to help him get the job done. Will this be the year Santa finally gets his Mrs. Klaus under the mistletoe?

About The Author

Katie Mettner

Katie Mettner writes small-town romantic tales filled with epic love stories and happily-ever-afters. She proudly wears the title of, 'the only person to lose her leg after falling down the bunny hill,' and loves decorating her prosthetic leg with the latest fashion trends. She lives in Northern Wisconsin with her own happily-ever-after and three mini-mes. Katie has a massive addiction to coffee and Twitter, and a lessening aversion to Pinterest — now that she's quit trying to make the things she pins.

A Note To My Readers

People with disabilities are just that—people. We are not 'differently abled' because of our disability. We all have different abilities and interests, and the fact that we may or may not have a physical or intellectual disability doesn't change that. The disabled community may have different needs, but we are productive members of society who also happen to be husbands, wives, moms, dads, sons, daughters, sisters, brothers, friends, and co-workers. People with disabilities are often disrespected and portrayed two different ways; as helpless or as heroically inspirational for doing simple, basic activities.

As a disabled author who writes disabled characters, my focus is to help people without disabilities understand the real-life disability issues we face like discrimination, limited accessibility, housing, employment opportunities, and lack of people first language. I want to change the way others see our community by writing strong characters who go after their dreams, and find their true love, without shying away from what it is like to be a person with a disability. Another way I can educate people without disabilities is to help them understand our terminology. We, as the disabled community, have worked to establish what we call People First Language. This isn't a case of being politically correct. Rather, it is a way to acknowledge and communicate with a person with a disability in a respectful way by eliminating generalizations, assumptions, and stereotypes.

As a person with disabilities, I appreciate when readers take the time to ask me what my preferred language is. Since so many have asked, I thought I would include a small sample of the people-first language we use in the disabled community. This language also applies when leaving reviews and talking about books that feature characters with disabilities. The most important thing to remember when you're talking to people with disabilities is that we are people first! If you ask us what our preferred terminology is regarding our disability, we will not only tell you, but be glad you asked! If you would like more information about people first language, you will find a disability resource guide on my website.

Instead of: He is handicapped.
Use: He is a person with a disability.

Instead of: She is differently abled.
Use: She is a person with a disability.

Instead of: He is mentally retarded.
Use: He has a developmental or intellectual disability.

Instead of: She is wheelchair-bound.
Use: She uses a wheelchair.

Instead of: He is a cripple.
Use: He has a physical disability.

Instead of: She is a midget or dwarf.
Use: She is a person of short stature or a little person.

Instead of: He is deaf and mute.
Use: He is deaf or he has a hearing disability.

Instead of: She is a normal or healthy person.
Use: She is a person without a disability.

Instead of: That is handicapped parking.
Use: That is accessible parking.

Instead of: He has overcome his disability.
Use: He is successful and productive.

Instead of: She is suffering from vision loss.
Use: She is a person who is blind or visually disabled.

Instead of: He is brain damaged.
Use: He is a person with a traumatic brain injury.

Other Books by Katie Mettner

The Fluffy Cupcake Series (2)

The Kontakt Series (2)

The Sugar Series (5)

The Northern Lights Series (4)

The Snowberry Series (7)

The Kupid's Cove Series (4)

The Magnificent Series (2)

The Bells Pass Series (5)

The Dalton Sibling Series (3)

The Raven Ranch Series (2)

The Butterfly Junction Series (2)

A Christmas at Gingerbread Falls

Someone in the Water (Paranormal)

White Sheets & Rosy Cheeks (Paranormal)

The Secrets Between Us

After Summer Ends (Lesbian Romance)

Finding Susan (Lesbian Romance)

Torched

Printed in Great Britain
by Amazon